Finn

7 Brides for 7 Brothers

JoAnn Ross

D1526040

Visit JoAnn's Website
www.joannross.com

Subscribe to JoAnn's newsletter
joannross.com/newsletter

Meet up with her on Facebook
facebook.com/JoAnnRossbooks

Follow her on Instagram
instagram.com/joannrossbooks

Also Available

7 Brides for 7 Brothers

Luke: Barbara Freethy (#1)
Gabe: Ruth Cardello (#2)
Hunter: Melody Anne (#3)
Knox: Christie Ridgway (#4)
Max: Lynn Raye Harris (#5)
James: Roxanne St. Clair (#6)
Finn: JoAnn Ross (#7)

Meet the Brannigan brothers—seven sexy brothers who bring the heart and the heat! From bestselling authors Barbara Freethy, Ruth Cardello, Melody Anne, Christie Ridgway, Lynn Raye Harris, Roxanne St. Claire and JoAnn Ross comes a brand-new contemporary romance family series: 7 Brides for 7 Brothers. You won't want to miss a single one!

FINN – JoAnn Ross

Finn Brannigan has a need for speed. Fast cars, fast jets, and the fast life that comes with being a TOPGUN aviator. He's flying missions over Afghanistan when his media mogul father dies unexpectedly, leaving Finn an airline in the wilds of the Alaskan wilderness. Which is a cool surprise, though he hasn't a clue what he's supposed to do with three small planes half a world away.

After escaping death—not once, but twice—Finn leaves the Navy and heads north to the Last Frontier to escape the world. But his planned isolation is blown to bits when he flies a runaway bride to her planned honeymoon cabin located in his remote mountain town of Caribou. As the short Alaskan summer spins out, Finn finds himself wanting to slow the days down and savor every delicious moment with the free-spirited singer/songwriter who's made him feel alive again.

Tori Cassidy has had it with dishonest, cheating playboys. Alaskan bush pilot Finn Brannigan is exactly the kind of man she can envision building a life with. Hardworking. Honest. Ordinary. There's just one problem: Finn is lying about who he really is.

Dedication

To the amazingly talented Jaspar Lepak, who not only wrote a beautiful song for Tori, but was also a joy to work with.

"Escape may be checked by land and by water, but the air and the sky are free."

Daedalus to Icarus

"You haven't seen a tree until you've seen its shadow from the sky."

Amelia Earhart

1

FINN BRANNIGAN HAD a need for speed. Fast cars, fast jets, and the fast life that came with being a naval aviator, the smallest, most elite—to his mind—club in the military. Which explained why he was about to commit a controlled crash, in the blackass dead of night, onto the pitching deck of an aircraft carrier after completing a bombing run of terrorist targets over Afghanistan.

A carrier landing was one of the most incredible rushes ever. But any pilot who didn't admit that a night one—significantly called a trap—out in the middle of a black ocean on a moonless night was also the most terrifying was flat-out lying.

It was like wearing a blindfold while flying through a bottle of ink dropped into the middle of a black hole, and all Finn had to do was pass over the ship, bank, pull off a three-to four-G high-level turn before bringing his jet in at full speed, hooking an arresting cable set four inches off the rolling, pitching deck that was running away from him.

Piece of cake, right?

Wrong.

Missing in any direction could not only mean the end of an aviator's career, it could prove fatal. Which was how Finn came to be sleeping in the rack of a guy who'd come up short and slammed his F/A-18 Hornet into the back of the *USS O'Halloran.*

As he approached the boat (and yeah, maybe sailors called the flattop a ship, but to aviators, anything that floated was a boat), Finn's heart kicked into high gear. Which was par for the course, since it had been proven aviators' pulse and blood pressure readings were higher when they were speeding up behind the carrier, preparing to snag one of four deck cables than while dodging surface-to-air missiles or flying in areas patrolled by enemy aircraft.

The weather had gotten worse. The blackened sea was pitching like crazy and the crosswinds had kicked up. Unfortunately, since they were too far out to sea to divert planes to the nearest bingo field—Navy speak for an alternate carrier land runway—he didn't have any other choice than to pull this landing off.

As he touched down onto the slanted deck hard enough to destroy lesser planes, Finn pushed the Hornet to full throttle, keeping power to become airborne in the off chance he missed a cable. Given that arrested landings were the most dangerous part of a dangerous business, even the best pilots could fly perfectly good aircraft into the sea.

He snagged the fourth and final cable and prepared his body for the shock of going from one hundred and fifty-five knots to a complete stop in under two seconds.

But the familiar, welcome jerk that would slam his body against the five-point harness with a force that had all his internal organs and head continuing to rush forward didn't happen. Instead, the jet merely slowed down and, as sailors scrambled for safety, careened down the landing deck. And if that weren't effed up enough, the drop in speed from having snagged the cable wouldn't allow Finn enough thrust to take off again. Which gave him seconds to eject.

Or...

There was one other possibility. Crazy, reckless, and perhaps suicidal.

Hell, like the Boss sang, *no retreat, no surrender*.

Deciding to go the fuck for broke, instead of hitting the eject button, Finn hung on and rode his fighter jet off the edge of the deck.

2

Ten months later
Caribou, Alaska

FOR AS FAR back as he could remember, flying had been Finn Brannigan's life. His older brothers still occasionally ragged him about having slept with toy planes when he was a toddler, and when other kids were coloring dinosaurs and houses with smiley suns, he'd been drawing pictures of Navy Phantoms and Tomcats.

During his years landing his F-18 Hornet onto carrier flight decks, Finn had had neither the time nor inclination to settle down with a wife, two-point-five kids, and a house with a picket fence. Like his former old-school TOPGUN commander had decreed, if the Navy had intended a naval aviator to have a spouse, they damn well would have issued him one.

During the past year, as if they'd all come down with the same virus, his six older brothers were now in committed relationships with their women. Hell, real estate tycoon Gabe had even gotten himself hitched! Fortunately, Finn had been inoculated against love at an early age.

Although Luke, Knox, and Max would probably never be entirely domesticated, from what he was able to tell, their lives had gotten a helluva lot more settled. And, hooyah for them, happier. But he still had every intention of remaining the last single Brannigan brother standing.

Colin Brannigan hadn't been military, but he might as well have been, given how much time he'd spent away from home running his media empire. Finn couldn't count the number of family events the old man had missed. Including both his and his brother Luke's twenty-first birthdays. At least he'd been away from the Naval Academy on a summer warship aviation training cruise. Not that he'd given a damn about whether or not the man even remembered his birthday. His assistant *had*, however, dutifully sent a snazzy, store-wrapped Burberry scarf, which would've gotten him thrown overboard if he'd dared shown up wearing it on a flight deck.

Luke, on the other hand, had been stood up at the restaurant after having been invited to a rare celebratory dinner. After a long wait, their father's assistant had called with the news (big effing surprise) that Colin had been called away on business, leaving the bartender to pour the

traditional coming-of-age Bushmills 21. The first
of many glasses, from what Finn had been able to
tell after his brother had called, drunk and
majorly pissed off. But, he'd sensed, deeply
disappointed.

Growing up watching his older brothers'
complex family relationships, Finn had long ago
decided that he had it easier. His memories of his
pretty blond mother were fleeting and vague, and
except for one memorable week-long trip with
Colin to Alaska the summer Finn turned thirteen,
his father had always been a distant, absent
parent.

All that, along with knowing that he'd only
been conceived as a final, last-ditch attempt to
have the daughter his mother had always wanted,
had taught Finn an early life lesson: it was easier
to keep from being wounded if he avoided
emotional entanglements in the first place.

He *had* come close once. He'd thought. Maybe. But the woman in question hadn't stuck
around long enough to find out. Which was
probably just as well.

After the initial shock, Finn hadn't been all
that surprised that his father had kept his fast-
moving cancer a secret from all his sons. The
media mogul had always lived his life to suit
himself, so it fit his personality to go out the same
way.

Finn *had* been stunned, however, to discover that he'd inherited Osprey Air, the three-plane airline in the remote town of Caribou, Alaska, he'd flown on during that trip with his dad. The highlight of the week had been when Mike Muldoon, the pilot/owner, had let him take the yoke as they'd soared over the craggy, snowy peaks of the central Alaska Range.

He'd learned of his father's death after that near carrier crash that, unfortunately, would probably remain on the Navy's YouTube channel forever. Hell, if he hadn't been the one in the cockpit having to pull off a maneuver that would go viral, he would've thought it cool to watch. Insane. But nevertheless cool.

His last-second decision, since ejecting at such a low altitude would've probably gotten him killed and sent his jet back to the taxpayers in pieces, had been to allow the plane to go ahead and fall toward the water, which, theoretically, should cause it to pick up speed. Fortunately, physics, and all the fates, had aligned, allowing him to go full throttle, fly back up again, and keep circling until the crews could clear the deck of debris and any injured from the cable snap. Then he'd landed again, this time snagging the second hook, leaving the third still available, just in case.

Once he'd been through the critique in the

Ready Room and had been both sharply and loudly dressed down for the risk and compliment-ed for pulling it off by his LSO, still too wired to sleep, he'd gone to the computer lab to check his email. Not that he'd expected any.

His family was a long way from the Waltons. The Brannigan brothers' email chain was a running joke, though he did occasionally receive extreme videos from Luke, who made big bucks in endorsements and those films. Finn had been hoping for one that night.

No such luck. Instead, the only thing in his inbox had been an email from his aunt Claire, which seemed a little odd since the weekly ones she'd always written while he was deployed usually showed up on Saturdays. The *Your Father* subject line also hadn't been encouraging. Although Finn and his father had never been close, news of his death had made an already sucky day even worse.

Nine months after receiving the email, after surviving being shot down by a surface-to-air-missile and spending two high-stressed nights in the Kush Mountains before being rescued by a team of kick-ass SEALs, he'd separated from the Navy and claimed his out-of-the-blue inheritance.

For the past month, instead of oceans and war-torn landscapes, he'd soared like an eagle over a vast, spectacular land that, from the air, looked like a three-dimensional Alaskan tourist bureau postcard. The snow-peaked mountains, dominated by Denali, were nothing short of majestic. And then there were the endless lakes. If Minnesota was the land of ten thousand lakes, which a pilot on his last carrier cruise had insisted, Alaska had to be the land of ten *million* lakes.

After taking a morning run along the lake the house he'd also inherited was situated on, he strolled into the office of Osprey Air, where Mary Muldoon had his daily flight schedule waiting for him. Mary was the widow of the pilot who'd taken him on those memorable flights so many years ago, and as far as anyone in the town of Caribou knew, she was still the owner. Finn was already a *cheechako*, a newcomer. No way did he want to show up in town as the guy who'd stolen a widow's livelihood out from under her.

After spending too many years trying avoid the media spotlight that followed Colin Brannigan around, Finn also intended to figuratively fly under the radar. The summer he'd come up here with his dad, he'd discovered Colin had used his wife's maiden name—Hayes—as an alias. He'd been surprised to discover that the high-profile media mogul occasionally just wanted to be seen as a regular guy. The way Finn did.

Even when his dad built the largest home in the valley—which wasn't nearly as expansive as the Calabasas ranch house the family called home—residents had merely viewed him as another rich guy who'd come to the last frontier for a remote getaway. To their minds, everyone in the lower forty-eight would probably love to do the same thing if they could afford it.

Then there was the third, most important reason Finn had kept the legacy secret. Having spent too many years crammed into four-bunk quarters on a carrier, and having escaped death not just once but twice, he wanted to be left alone and savor the peace and quiet. Fortunately, along with keeping track of the schedules, accounting books, and payroll, Mary actually enjoyed chatting with people.

When Finn had first learned of his inheritance, he'd tried to sign it over to her, but she'd refused, insisting that his father had obviously intended for him to have it, so who was she to argue with a man's last wishes? As far as he was concerned, she might not be the owner, but she was the boss. And his ego didn't have a problem with that.

"Good morning!" Her smile was, as always, as wide as a half-moon. Although it wasn't yet seven in the morning, long black hair streaked with silver was already tumbling from a messy bun atop her head. "You've got a party of two on a flight out of Anchorage," she said, handing him a

Thermos of steaming coffee. The woman brewed a better joe than he'd ever gotten from the carrier mess, which had gained a Starbucks before his last cruise.

"They're not taking the train or bus?"

Tourists took over Caribou in the summer, coming up to visit Denali National Park, hike, fish, and just soak in the magnificence of nature. Many came to attempt to climb the highest mountain in North America, and Osprey Air made a good living catering to all of them. But Finn had yet to run into any tourist who'd actually ponied up the big bucks to fly here from Anchorage.

"The guy's on his honeymoon, so I guess he wants to spare no expense to impress his bride."

"Seems there are a lot better ways to impress your bride on a honeymoon than throw around money," he said.

"It's been fifty some years since my wedding night, but I'd have to agree with you on that." She handed him the clipboard with the name and flight from Seattle's arrival time.

"Carter George Covington IV?"

"Yeah. It's a mouthful, isn't it? Seems the family isn't exactly known for originality when it comes to naming their kids."

"The Covingtons are big on tradition. And status."

She lifted a brow. "Sounds like you know of them."

"They own Covington Cruise Lines out of L.A. As well as a bunch of hotels. I don't know them well, but they'd show up at my family's annual Christmas open house. Carter's a few years older than me, but he was a bratty kid who, last time I saw him, had grown into a dick of a teenager."

"Small world," she said.

"Tell me about it. Dad must have mentioned flying Osprey on his trips up here to Carter III, which was probably how we got to be the lucky ones IV chose." Finn couldn't keep the distaste from his voice.

"You want me to give the flight to Yazz?" Jim Yazzie was a native Alaskan who'd flown jets for the Air Force before returning to his hometown to fly for Osprey.

"Nah. He said something about a cousin's birthday." Which, given the size of the Yazzie family, could include half the town. "I don't mind taking it."

Her brown eyes narrowed as both expressive gray brows dove toward her nose. "You'll be on your best behavior, right?"

For not the first time, Finn recognized that Osprey was closer to Mary's heart than it was his. Which was why, to his mind, it would always be a

Muldoon airline. He lifted his right hand. "I'll be a perfect officer and gentleman."

After all, being on their honeymoon, the groom and his bride surely had better things to do than talk to a bush pilot. Who, Finn figured, Covington would consider nothing more than a glorified bus driver. No, a *mere* driver. Like the chauffeur who always drove him to and from that ritzy prep school his parents had sent him to. They'd probably wanted to keep him away as much as possible. If there was ever a kid even his mother couldn't like, it had to be IV.

"What's the bride's name?" he asked.

"Her ticket's in the name of Tori Cassidy. Covington booked the flight last month, so he went with her maiden name."

"Cassidy?"

"Another old acquaintance?" Damn. That was a downside to working with Mary. No nuance, however small, got past her radar. She'd obviously picked up on his surprise.

"The name sounds familiar." Finn faked a shrug. "Covington might have brought her along to the party once. Or maybe she's rich herself and showed up with her family. God knows, since Dad invited seemingly every one of the one-percenters he'd ever done business with to the open house, the place was packed to the rafters."

Which was hard to do, given that the Brannigan family Calabasas Canyon ranch house was huge even for SoCal standards. Colin Brannigan had never been one to shy away from ostentation.

The truth, which he had no intention of sharing, was that Tori Cassidy was a blast from Finn's not-so-distant past. And while, granted, they hadn't spent much time talking that night they'd spent together, she hadn't seemed to be a gold digger. Which was the only reason he could think of why any sane woman would marry a douche like Carter George Covington IV.

3

TORI CASSIDY'S HEART kicked into overdrive
when she saw Finn Brannigan, of all people,
in the baggage area of Anchorage's Ted Stevens
International Airport. Standing with other locals
she guessed were drivers and pilots, he was
holding up a sign reading *Covington*. Surely—
please God—he couldn't be the pilot Carter had
hired to fly them to their honeymoon cabin.

Her life had bottomed out the past twenty-
four hours, but fate couldn't be that cruel. Could
it? When he put the phone he was talking on back
into his pocket, then lifted a brow and looked
straight at her, she decided that if fate wasn't
cruel, it had a damn sardonic sense of humor.

The scruff of beard—which he hadn't had
that hot Coronado night they'd spent together—
was new. As were the tight black T-shirt, brown
leather jacket, and snug jeans faded in all the right
places that looked even hotter than the Navy dress
whites she'd been in such a hurry to strip off him.

Not that he needed to wear a uniform to stand out in the crowd. There was no way anyone could miss his six feet two inches of ultimate alpha male. Nor his piercing agate eyes and jaw wide enough to land his fighter jet on. Both his short haircut and squared away, broad-shouldered stance shouted military.

It took every ounce of fortitude Tori possessed not to take a step backwards as he headed toward her. Just as he had that night, as she'd watched him make his way across the crowded dance floor of the Hotel del Coronado ballroom. He certainly hadn't been the top-ranked male in the room of uniforms covered in various medals and battle ribbons, but as she'd watched from the stage, people had parted, giving him an open path as he zeroed straight in on his target. Which had been her.

It was currently high tourist season in Alaska, and the baggage claim area was packed with travelers. All who unconsciously reacted the way those dancers had. While the SEALs might be the rock stars of the Navy, aviators were the royalty. The way Finn strode toward her with the air of confidence Carter had never been able to pull off, even in his forty-thousand-dollar Brioni suits, demonstrated that he'd never expect any mere mortal to dare stand in his way.

With his gaze locked on hers, they could have

been the only two people in the terminal. Her heart kicked up even higher, not quite to a full-blown attack, but definitely into fight-or-flight mode. Since, unfortunately, she had no place to go, nor the money to get there, Tori placed her hand on her hip and slipped into the sassy, got-it-all-together girl mode she'd acquired to hide her insecurities. And, in some cases, fear.

"Well, hello, Sailor," she said, throwing in a toss of her dark hair for good measure to keep him from noticing that her knees were shaking. "Fancy seeing you here."

The only hint that he wasn't exactly thrilled by being referred to as a *sailor* was a slight tightening at the corner of his right eye. His expression stayed as neutral as it had been when he'd invited her to his suite for a drink after she'd finished her last set. Having been living in Southern California at the time, Tori had dated enough military guys to have heard the claim that carrier aviators had ice water in their veins. Which she supposed had to be true, considering the risks they took. But by the time dawn was filtering into the suite's bedroom window, that ice had not just melted, it had flamed into molten lava.

"Your groom hired me to fly you to Caribou." He glanced around. "Where is he?"

"I suppose back home in Los Angeles," she said.

If he was surprised she'd come to Alaska alone, he didn't show it. Oh, yes, the ice shield was back. Which, Tori told herself, was a good thing. She'd come up here to get away, write her songs, and figure out the next stage of her life. Not to have a fling with a hotshot flyboy, even one who'd given her the best sex she'd ever experienced.

"That's my bag." Before she could grab the suitcase as it came rumbling by, he'd scooped it off the carousel.

"You're traveling light. Is this all you've got?"

"That and my Taylor." She'd carried the guitar on both planes with her. After having lived on ramen and taco truck takeout for six months to pay for it, no way was she going to risk the airline losing it. "I hadn't intended to stay that long."

"You might find yourself changing your mind. This place has a way of taking hold of you in a way that's almost mystical."

"I'm not one to settle down," she said.

"A rolling stone," he reminded her what she'd told him that night. "Which seems an oxymoron with marriage."

"Not every marriage includes a picket fence," she said, hating that she sounded so defensive.

"We're in perfect agreement there. I flew another runaway bride just last week," he said conversationally as they headed toward the door leading out of the terminal. "Home to Juneau. She'd gotten cold feet."

"My feet are just fine, thank you."

He glanced down at them as they walked toward several channels with floatplanes tied to docks. "I remember them being a lot better than fine."

Tori so didn't need this trip down memory lane. While he hadn't gone as far as to suck her toes, while tasting every bit of her body—which she'd buffed and polished for one of the better-paying gigs of her roller-coaster career—he *had* pressed a long, hot, wet kiss on the arch of each foot, which she'd discovered were directly connected to her girly parts, which had broken into a happy dance.

"Nice boots, by the way," he said.

"Thank you."

Having been forced to move around as much as she had, and later by choice, Tori had learned a lot about how to blend into her surroundings. To fit in without entirely giving up her individuality. Except for those four years she wasn't going to think about. Ever. Again.

Still, if she was going to spend her honeymoon in the wilds of Alaska instead of lying on some sundrenched beach having cabana boys bring her fruity tropical drinks served in coconuts with pretty little umbrellas, she'd been determined not to look as if she'd joined the infantry. After an extensive online search, she'd settled on these, which weren't pretty, but at least they were bright red. Unfortunately, during the flights from Los Angeles to Seattle, then Seattle to Anchorage, they'd already begun rubbing against her little toe.

"I can show you how to stretch out that right boot. Or I know a guy who'll do it for you."

Another thing that hadn't changed. Aviators were reputed to have the eyes of eagles. He certainly hadn't missed any part of her body, or any reaction, no matter how nuanced, to his lovemaking.

Not lovemaking, she reminded herself. It had been just sex. Hot, chandelier-swinging, dirty sex. It had also been so mind-blowing that sometime during the night, she'd realized that Lieutenant Finn Brannigan, USN, had ruined her for any other man. Which had only been one of the reasons she'd gotten dressed and crept out of his suite that morning before he could wake up.

"They fit fine," she lied. The four-inch stilettos she'd been wearing the night they'd met had been more comfortable. These felt as if she'd laced concrete blocks onto her feet. Then there was that hot spot she could feel turning into a blister. Hence the limp he'd obviously noticed. "I don't intend to do a lot of hiking while I'm here."

"Too bad." He put his free hand lightly on

her lower back, not, she determined, to make a move but simply to shepherd her to where he'd wanted her to go. The way he had as they'd left the ballroom to the elevator. Where, once the doors had closed behind them, he'd kissed her breathless. "There's a lot of wilderness to explore up here. So, what are your plans, now that it sounds as if the wedding's off the table?"

Good question. "My plans are rather up in the air at the moment. I figured I'd wing it." A stiff breeze off the water was churning her hair into a wild tangle. "Take things one day at a time," she said as she tried to hold it back from her face with her free hand.

"Good for you." He flashed his movie star straight, white teeth in a sexy smile that should come with a warning label. "See, you're already getting into the spirit of this place. I got up this morning expecting to help some senior couple check another item off their bucket list by flying them to a glacier. And here I am with you." After putting on the Ray-Bans he'd hooked into the neck of that T-shirt, he dug into the pocket of his jacket and pulled out a strip of leather which he handed to her.

"Thanks." Thinking that he seemed to always prepared for anything, like those condoms he'd just happened to handily have with him, she put down the guitar case long enough to tie the flying curls into a semblance of a messy tail. "Life can definitely be unpredictable."

"That's for damn sure."

There was a sudden, unexpected edge to his tone that didn't fit their outwardly casual conversation. There was something there, Tori considered. Something that might explain what he was doing here in the Last Frontier instead of flying off an aircraft carrier somewhere dangerous. Or even in Nevada, teaching a new class of Topgun pilots, as he'd told her he'd been doing when temporarily assigned to San Diego to coordinate his old commander's retirement party.

After walking along the floating dock, which she had to admit was better suited to these clunky boots than all the pretty high heels she'd left back in L.A., he stopped in front of a red-and-white plane that had been pulled up onto a wooden ramp, its tail pointed toward the water.

Yikes. While she didn't want to disparage the plane, it looked, well, *chunky*. No, that was putting it politely. She had trouble believing this huge, hulking aircraft could actually get airborne.

"This must be quite a change for you," she said.

"You mean a downgrade," he corrected easily as he opened a compartment and stowed her suitcase.

"Well, it's not exactly a fighter jet."

Despite a lust level that should have set off earthquake shake alerts all over Southern California, they had actually taken breaks to talk during that night. She'd told him about some of her more colorful gigs, sticking to the good stuff, while he'd waxed so romantically about his Hornet he might as well have been talking about another woman.

"The de Havilland Beaver just happens to be *the* iconic Alaskan bush plane," he informed her with obvious pride. And, she realized, affection. "There are also a lot of pilots who dream of a chance to fly it, and others have been known to take their hats off when one flies over. Just seeing it in the air can be a religious experience."

"I'm all in favor of freedom of religion." But revering a plane, especially one that looked as if it belonged in an animated cartoon movie, seemed to be carrying things a bit far.

"Harrison Ford owns one."

"I seem to remember him crashing," Tori said.

"Not in this baby." He ran his hand over the side of the gigantic plane, in much the way he'd stroked his way down her back while unzipping the red, white, and blue sequined dress she'd gotten from Rent the Runway for the occasion. "That was a 1942 Ryan Aeronautical ST3KR."

The man obviously knew his planes. Still…

"It might look like a tank, but she flies like a Harley with wings," he reassured her.

"And that's a good thing?"

After the way Carter had tricked and betrayed her, Tori had convinced herself that she deserved to take advantage of this already-paid-for honeymoon. Now she was beginning to second-guess the idea. In her mind, she and Carter would have been flying on a smaller version of his luxurious private jet with its uniformed pilot and flight attendant.

"Why do I get the feeling you don't think my floatplane's sexy?"

The question was an all-too-obvious play on the Kenny Chesney song she'd satirized that night changing the original "tractor" to "She thinks my flattop's sexy," a reference to the carrier fleet for which the retiring commander had spent so many years training pilots. Including Lieutenant Finn Brannigan.

"Trust me." And wasn't that exactly what he'd said that night when she'd told him she wasn't in the habit of going to hotel rooms with strangers? "This is the best plane in the business for float work. Weather gets dicey up here and can change dramatically on a dime. One minute you can be soaring over mountaintops with nothing but blue skies ahead. The next you can be facing a thick gray wall that obscures everything on your flight path. That's when you want a big, tough aircraft that can eat Cessnas and Super Cubs like they're bar peanuts."

"An interesting simile," she murmured. "But it still doesn't look very fast. For a guy who's into speed."

"True enough. But the feeling of speed doesn't exist when you're in the air, which is why being a passenger in an airliner can be so boring."

"I can feel airliners going fast on takeoff."

"That's thrust. Totally different thing."

"I'll have to take your word for that... So." She looked a long way up to the door. Fortunately, a metal ladder was attached to the float. "It's very high."

His mouth curved. "It's a bit of a climb. But Osprey Air provides full service. I can climb up behind you and give you a boost."

That's all she needed. This man's large, wickedly clever hands on her butt. "Thanks. But I'm sure I can manage it."

"Okay. Just be careful not to step on any of that green algae with those pretty new boots or you'll land on your ass and slide into the water."

"And wouldn't that round off a perfect week?" she muttered.

"Let me at least help you to the ladder."

Since she was going to have to walk along that big, missile-shaped pontoon, Tori reminded herself that her pride would be a great deal more injured if she slid into the water, so she allowed him to hold her arm as together they made their way to the ladder. After climbing up with a serious lack of grace, she squeezed through the door that seemed awfully narrow for such a big plane and, exhaling a deep breath, settled into the passenger seat. Where she sat, safely buckled in, hands squeezed tightly together, watching as Finn did his outside preflight check.

He seemed methodical, which she'd expect for a pilot of his expertise. Which again had her wondering what he was doing all the way up here in Alaska, flying her from an already remote airport out into an even more distant location. There was a story there. But then again, didn't she have a few of her own, which she wasn't prepared to share?

Surprisingly, he pushed the plane into the water, which had it floating away about ten feet from the ramp. Terrific. Fearing that she was destined to be stuck inside alone as it floated out to sea, she watched him yank a long line, spinning the Beaver around so the tail was now pointed toward the ramp.

He pulled it back in until it just slid onto the planking, then, in what appeared to be a tricky maneuver requiring a great deal of finesse, he walked along the left float, as she'd done on the right, then climbed in.

"Doing okay?" he asked. The testosterone coming off him in waves filled the cockpit and probably raised the heat level a good ten degrees.

"Just dandy," she assured him as her head swam. "Of course, that could be because we're still on the ground. Or, more precisely, water." They were drifting away from the dock. "Please tell me this thing has good brakes."

"Actually, it doesn't have any."

"None?" she asked on what, dammit, sounded more like a squeak than her normal voice.

"Nope. Which I'd been told, but the first time I flew one, I nearly jammed the rudder pedals through the floor trying to slow down when a Cessna zipped across my path."

"How do you stop if you don't have brakes?"

There were so many planes docked, many with passengers and pilots loading onto them. A songwriter had to have a good imagination, and Tori's was now picturing herself caught in the middle of a floatplane demolition derby. In water that, although it was technically summer, was probably glacier cold.

"If you've already started the engine, you can reduce taxiing speed by throttling back. In the case of the Cessna, I just turned circles until it passed. If you're going into the wind, which we're not today, you can lower the flaps or open the doors to make more surface for the wind to blow against, which reduces speed."

"Open the doors?"

He smiled. Rather indulgently, she thought. As if he were dealing with a six-year-old. Who, thinking about it, would probably love the idea of flying with the doors open. She did not.

"Like I said, you don't have to worry. If we do have to stop once we get started, I can just shut off the engine and the friction of the water will stop us. The Beaver flies like a wheeled plane when you're in the air. But right now, we're essentially on a boat."

Tori would rather be on dry land. She'd seen a ticket booth in the terminal for both trains and buses to Caribou. That's what she should have done. This taking off business was bad enough. If she was going to have to fly into the wilderness in this bulky, winged boxcar, she'd feel a lot better knowing they were at least going to land on solid ground.

"Your former fiancé paid big bucks for this ride. It'd be a shame if you didn't enjoy it."

"Good point." With Taylor Swift's "Shake it Off" playing in her head, she drew in a deep breath, blew it out, and literally shook her shoulders. "I'm ready for takeoff, Captain."

"It's Lieutenant. And that's the most encouraging thing I've heard all day."

His baritone dropped deeper. Turned smoother. Not quite into Barry White bass mode, but enough to have every erogenous zone in her body perking up with interest. "I was speaking in regards to the aircraft."

"Too bad."

She drew back as the air shifted when he leaned closer, both afraid and hoping that he'd kiss her the way he had in the hotel elevator. Instead, he was merely doing something piloty to one of the doohickies on the control panel that looked like it might have been taken from some early spacecraft. Maybe the one John Glenn had orbited the earth in. She'd seen *Friendship 7* in the Smithsonian during the six months she'd lived in D.C. and had marveled that anyone would ever be willing to squeeze himself into a human sardine can and go rocketing off into space.

Which brought up a question she knew enough not to ask him while he was busy preparing for takeoff. Besides, she still had a few Hail Marys to get through.

The engine started with a rumble, which had Tori feeling vibrations in already stimulated body parts. But any sexy thoughts were blown away by the deafening roar as the plane went shooting across the water, sending up spray against the windshield, causing sea gulls to scatter out of the way, and—thank you, God!—became airborne.

"You're going to miss a lot of cool scenery if you keep your eyes closed." Finn's tone was mild, but his deep voice held humor that she found both annoying and too appealing for her own good.

He'd affected her that way from the beginning. A man so confident could be conceited. But he hadn't proven to be, and while he'd made her moan as they tangled the sheets, he'd also made her laugh. Which had been another first.

"Easy for you to say since you're the one holding on to the steering wheel," she shot back, even as she opened her eyes and stared at the mountains soaring into a blindingly blue sky. She'd seen them flying into the airport, but somehow, in this loud, ugly (well, to her) plane, she felt as if she could reach out and touch them.

"Yoke." He took one hand off the half wheel, reached across the wide console, and unwound her clenched fingers. "A steering wheel on a plane is a yoke. Or stick. And you should have told me you're a white-knuckle flier."

"I'm not. Usually. But until this, the smallest plane I've ever been in was a twelve-seat puddle jumper from Charlotte to Myrtle Beach."

"You get around," he said.

"That's me," she said as she reclaimed her hand. Her loss, but she didn't want him to get the wrong idea. She was only here for solitude and songwriting. Not for any funny business. Now, if only she could get her body, which was all too aware of him, on board with that plan. "A gypsy rover."

"Do you whistle, too?"

Once again he'd surprised her. "You know the song?" Which, while usually thought of as "Gypsy Rover," was actually titled "The Whistling Gypsy."

"Hey, I'm Irish. The first time I heard it was when the Clancy Brothers covered it. And you mentioning it caused a flash of memory of singing it on a family road trip. I was in a minivan with my mom and three of my brothers—Gabe, Luke, and Knox. My other three brothers rode with Dad."

"There are seven of you?" She tried to imagine all that male hotness and testosterone in one place. "Your mom must've been Wonder Woman."

"I don't remember much about her since she died when I was four. I do remember her singing. And fishing. She taught me to bait my own hook.

"Anyway, she loved to sing along with the car radio. Luke, who's three years older than I am, once said that she didn't have that great a voice, but all I know is that it made me happy when she'd sing. It was like sunshine on a cloudy day."

"I'm sorry about your mother."

And didn't she know how that felt? Tori wondered how his mother had died. And what had happened to the family after that. To his dad and all those brothers, but decided that asking might open up questions about her own parents.

That was a personal story she'd never shared with anyone. Which was why it was so ironic that Carter, who'd been the only man to know her life history firsthand, had been the one who'd taken such malicious advantage of it.

"I was sorry, too," he said. "Not so much at the time, because I don't think I was old enough to understand the concept of death being forever. Later, I wondered how different things would've been if she'd lived."

She had to ask. "And now?"

"I don't." His eyes, hidden behind the aviator shades, gave nothing away, but the curtness in his tone declared that topic closed. Which was fine with her.

"The Clancy Brothers and the Temptations," she murmured, having picked up on the sunshine and cloudy day line. "You have eclectic tastes."

"I can't carry a tune, but I like music," he said. "Your voice was the first thing that caught my attention."

"Really?"

She'd blown her hair into a sexy cloud, poured herself into a flag-colored sequined dress, and had gone heavy with a smoky eye, which was not her usual, more country/folk-singer style but fit the venue, and he'd overlooked all that for her voice? Which, she guessed, was a compliment. Of sorts.

"I had to leave the Crown Room to take a call right before the banquet ended," he said. "I heard you singing as I walked across the lobby to the ballroom."

"And I sounded like sunshine?"

"No. You sounded like all the things that go through a guy's head when he imagines getting a woman naked and heating up some sheets."

"Oh." She was pretty sure that was a move. Did he really think just because fate had thrown them together again, she'd be willing to start up where they'd left off?

Although Finn Brannigan was hot sex on a stick, that wasn't what she'd come here for. She was here to figure out what to do with her life. Where to go next. And to write a my-record-company-went-bankrupt, my-fiancé-was-a-lying-cheating-douche, and now-I'm-flat-broke blues ballad that could possibly get her back into the game. *If* she could find a recording company willing to take her on after the bankruptcy debacle.

When he turned the steering wheel—yoke—and headed away from Anchorage, Tori couldn't decide which was going to be more dangerous. Getting up over those enormous, craggy, snowcapped mountains, or that ignored topic they'd eventually have to talk about. Especially now that he'd brought up those hot sheets. Which had mostly ended up on the carpet.

"Speaking of the blue whale in the cockpit," he said, as if he'd developed superpower mind-reading ability, "we're going to have to talk about it."

"I believe that saying refers to elephants." Tori wasn't going to deny she knew he was talking about that night and, probably more specifically, the morning after, but she could try sidetracking the conversation.

"You're in Alaska now," he said. "Where everything's bigger. A blue whale can weigh in at two hundred tons. Which just happens to be the combined weight of thirty elephants."

"Thank you for the Wikipedia Infogram. I'll store it away in case I ever find myself trapped at a really boring cocktail party. And as interesting as it might admittedly be, there's really nothing we have to talk about."

"How about you sneaking out after using me for sex all night?"

Using him? Seriously? "I don't remember you complaining about being taken advantage of."

"The sex was totally mutual. It was the next

morning when you took unilateral action."

"Now you're talking like a military manual."

"I may not be active anymore, but I'm still IRR. Which technically makes me military."

"And IRR is?"

"Individual Ready Reserve. Which requires mustering once a year."

"That makes it sound as if you're going off to join up with General Washington to cross the Delaware."

"I guess it does. But it isn't an actual physical muster. I just need to send in a screening certificate. And remain ready and able to mobilize if required…. And you're dodging the subject."

"Okay." She huffed out a breath. "I knew you had a busy day following the banquet and ball, when you were supposed to lead that base tour for all the families who'd shown up for your commander's party. I figured you needed your sleep."

"That'd be considerate if it were true. And, for the record, I was awake when you sneaked out."

She'd been looking out over the ice fields and hundreds of small, blindingly blue sparkling lakes. Not only was the scenery stunning, it also kept her from having to meet his gaze. But that statement got her attention. She turned back toward him.

"You were not awake."

"I damn well was. And by the way, that scarlet-as-sin thong you were crawling around the floor looking for was on top of the lampshade."

He laughed as she blushed. Which she never did. Except, dammit, with this man. She'd done a lot of things with Finn Brannigan she'd never done before. But that was then and this is now, and since the Caribou website claimed the town had a total population of six hundred and twenty-four, making it next to impossible to keep from running into him, she was just going to have to be strong. Confident. And never let him see her sweat. She'd be every bit as cool and in control as Katniss Everdeen in the arena.

At least, she hoped, as he tipped those shades down his nose and gave her a hot, I-know-you-want-my-manly-body look, cool enough to keep from melting into a little puddle of lust before they landed.

4

O F ALL THE charter airlines flying in Alaska, Tori Cassidy just had to end up in his. Finn had come to Alaska not just to claim that surprising legacy his father had left him but because he'd wanted to be alone and avoid any personal entanglements. Being up in the sky had always released both his mind and his body from being tethered to the ground. Alone in the cockpit, he had no one to answer to other than the forces of Mother Nature.

From the time he'd gotten his pilot's license at thirteen, the sky had become like Finn's cathedral. A hushed place he could be alone to ponder the vagaries of the universe, which, in earlier years, admittedly revolved more around girls and getting past third base, which it took him another three years to achieve.

Here he could drink in the beauty of this wild land, which was so different from the dry California mountains he'd grown up in or the flat expanse of ocean he'd spent the past years flying over. He could also, if he chose, turn up his iPhone and belt out the Boss's "Born to Run" at the top of his lungs. Which was why, although he never would have expected to enjoy flying freight, he actually preferred it to passengers.

Crates of milk, canned vegetables, and toilet paper didn't need to have glaciers and native animals straight out of *Wild Kingdom* pointed out to them. They didn't need to be chatted up so they'd give him a good evaluation at the end of the flight. Not that he was in danger of getting fired, considering he owned Osprey, but in his former business, failure to shoot for perfection could get you killed. So far, he'd managed to get nearly all tens. Except for one damn nine, which he still didn't think he deserved since the family's airsick ten-year-old had hurled all over the dad's pants instead of the airsick bag Finn had handed out to everyone preflight.

If he'd believed in fate, Finn might have thought Tori showing up out of the blue had been predestined. Although he'd seen guys killed and had almost died himself, twice, Finn had never thought all that much about the afterlife. When you put your life on the line every time you climbed into a fighter jet's cockpit, pondering the ramifications of death could only be a distraction.

Still, he couldn't deny that the legacy each of

his brothers had received from their father had changed their lives. Luke, who'd taught him to rock climb, was now not only engaged but was about to become a stepfather to his college girlfriend's teenage niece. Real estate tycoon Gabe had surprised everyone with an out-of-the-blue wedding on the family ranch last October, and Hunter's treasure map had taken him on an adventure that had culminated in love. Knox, who'd been as much into hit-and-run relationships as Finn himself was, had inherited a classic old Indian motorcycle, which had led him to a yoga girl who must have taught him some amazing new moves, because damned if he hadn't put a ring on it, too.

And who'd have believed that his tough-guy Navy SEAL brother Max, of all people, would've settled down in Kentucky horse country with a woman who didn't even raise Thoroughbreds for racing, but something called an American saddlebred? Which, when Finn had Googled it, admittedly looked pretty cool, but he'd give his left nut to see Max in camos high-step prancing around an arena on the back of one.

Finn suspected their dad had his own reasons for giving the only one of them who didn't drink wine a small Italian winery. Had he known Mr. Perfect former altar boy, it's-all-about-the-bottom-line James would fall under the spell of a dolce vita and tumble into love and get engaged?

Although he wasn't involved in the family business the way James had always been, Finn had never known Colin Brannigan not to make long-range plans. Unless it came to his kids, in which cases, his attention tended to be hit-and-miss.

Finn didn't care about the ranch or the winery. Or any of the legacies any of his other brothers had been given. Though he wouldn't mind if, when Gabe and his bride started populating the ranch with a new generation that would require the acquisition of a minivan, he might consider passing on that limited edition Aston Martin of his.

Because while he'd never envied his brother's fancy Italian suits and shoes or bank account, he couldn't deny lusting after a ride that that would go zero to sixty in three-point-five seconds. Maybe once winter set in and flying slowed down, he'd take a trip to California. Check out the new bride and test out Gabe's Aston Martin. Just the thought of racing around the hairpin turns of the Santa Monica Mountains, where the Brannigans' Calabasas ranch was located, had him smiling.

"Something funny?"

"Just thinking about stuff," he said.

When she didn't ask what, exactly, had been on his mind, and turned her gaze back out the passenger window, he figured she was afraid he'd bring up that night again.

"Do you believe in an afterlife?"

"Why?" Color fled her cheeks. Cheekbones that could cut glass drew his eyes up to gypsy dark eyes that had a sexy, catlike slant to them. At the moment, they were widened with a fear he'd never understand but had come to recognize since he'd begun flying civilians. "Are you planning to crash anytime soon?"

"No. I was just wondering about whether or not people actually end up somewhere after they die."

"Brannigan," she murmured, not directly speaking to the question. "That's Irish, right?"

"Yeah, it is."

"So, you grew up Catholic?"

"We were. My older brother, a.k.a. James the Perfect, was even an altar boy. By the time I was old enough to serve, we'd pretty much lapsed except for Christmas. Mom was the one who'd drag us to mass."

Tori's fruity, floral scent surrounding them in the close confines of the cockpit smelled like Italy in a bottle, reminding him of a memorable shore leave in Naples when the *O'Halloran* had been taking part in Green Fleet exercises off the coast of Italy. Since somehow, they'd gotten off talking about masses, her perfume or lotion or whatever it was had his mind drifting to thoughts of what the nun who'd taught his first communion class had probably meant when she kept talking about avoiding a near occasion of sin.

At the time, Finn had figured Sister Bartholomew had been talking about cussing or like when they'd been at that resort back when his mom was still alive and he'd hid Hunter's baseball glove beneath some straw in a stable stall after his older brother, who just happened to be Gabe's twin, told him that he was too young to play baseball with the "big boys." Unfortunately, he was busted when one of the trail horses found it and chewed through the laces.

Finn couldn't remember much about that day, but by the time Sister Bartholomew entered his life—and for some weird reason had stayed on to become the voice of his conscience—he'd been ragged about it enough times by Hunter for him to decide he'd better list it with his more frequent sins he had to share at his first confession. A short list topped by sassing his latest demon of a nanny his father had hired to wrangle his seven sons. A job Finn had later come to realize was probably on the level of corralling a herd of wild mustangs.

What he'd done with Tori Cassidy that night at the Del had been no sin. Just the opposite. If it wasn't a freaking miracle, it had come damn close. She'd touched him, deep down, in some inexplicable way that nearly had him hearing an entire choir of angels singing "Hallelujah." It had been both the most amazing and frightening experience of Finn's life.

Even more terrifying, in a way, than when he'd been forced to eject to avoid getting turned to toast by that SAM over Afghanistan. At least he'd been well trained to handle *that* situation.

During that night with Tori, as he'd felt the fissures cracking in that wall of ice he'd spent a lifetime building around his heart, he'd entered unknown territory. It had been like falling into a black hole. The same as the spatial disorientation, the conflict between what the eyes see and the body feels that pilots could experience and what caused a majority of crashes.

He'd definitely lost all connection with his horizon that night. And he'd feared, as he'd drifted off to sleep, uncharacteristically contented with her dark head on his chest, he'd also lost his vigilantly guarded heart.

Then the next morning, through slitted eyes, he'd watched her take off. Proving what he'd already known.

Everyone leaves.

"My parents died when I was young," she volunteered into the silence that had settled over them.

"Really?" Their conversation that night hadn't ventured into anything that serious. "Both of them? How old were you?"

"Eleven. They died in a car accident in Hawaii. A tourist drank too many mai tais at a Maui resort luau and crossed the center line on a mountain curve."

As Finn knew well from attending too many boots-and-helmet memorial services, death was always out there, stalking even the bravest and toughest. Friends he'd lost in war, his mom he barely remembered, and more recently, his dad he'd hardly known.

"That must've been tough. Were you with them?"

"No. They'd flown down there from L.A. to open up a house in Kapalua for the family they worked for. They'd only expected to stay there a few days and I was in school."

Since his own family had a vacation home, which they seldom ever went to, in that area, Finn knew that homes there could easily go into the double-digit millions. Which, because the Covingtons had a place on the bay, gave him an uneasy feeling about who her parents might have been working for.

The last time he'd been to the Brannigan gated Maui estate had been over New Year's during his plebe year at the Academy. He'd spent three days surfing on nearby Honolulu Bay and regretting that Knox, who'd taught him to surf on that beach, hadn't been there to tackle those fifteen-foot swells.

"Do you have brothers? Sisters?" Although his might not be the closest of families—okay, they could occasionally verge on dysfunctional—he knew that any of his brothers would always have his six.

"No, I was an only child."

Finn had always felt like the Brannigan afterthought, treated like a cub in a pack where bonds had been formed and roles claimed before he'd been born. But he'd never been as alone as he imagined an eleven-year-old orphan must have been.

"But you did have other family?"

"No. My parents married late, so my grandparents had already passed on. And they were only children, too, so…"

Her voice trailed off. She sounded a little lost. Memories, he knew all too well, could come barreling back to roll over you when you least expected them. Like your plane falling off a flight deck, or ejecting from your cockpit into terrorists' no-man's land.

"We don't have to talk about it if you don't want to."

She shook her head. "No. It's okay. It was a long time ago. Eighteen years, actually. And, as you can see, I'm doing just fine. But to answer your question, I have no idea what happens after we die, but I do like imagining my parents watching over me. Which is why I try so hard to make them proud."

Bolting her wedding suggested that she wasn't exactly doing just fine, but Finn wasn't going to quibble. "I'm sure, if they are watching, they're damn proud. And from where I'm sitting, you're a helluva lot better than fine." He lowered his voice to a low, sexy drawl.

"You're hitting on me again."

"Hard not to," he said truthfully.

Finn wondered what had happened to Tori Cassidy, where, without any immediate family to count on, she'd spent the seven years between her parents' deaths, and when she would've reached legal age and gone out into the world all alone. But that conversation could wait for another time. After all, the cabin was paid up for two weeks.

Which brought up another question. Would Covington come after her? Finn hadn't when she'd left *him*. He'd also regretted that lapse more than once.

"You're definitely going to shake things up in Caribou," he predicted, deciding he didn't want to waste time alone with a beautiful woman thinking about death. "Women are in the minority in this state, especially up where we're headed, so expect to get hit on a lot."

She shrugged. "I can handle myself. You've no idea how many guys figure a girl who stands up on stage in the spotlight every night is just looking for a good time." She flashed that smile he'd been waiting for. "Though women don't tend to get groupies like guys. Especially drummers."

"I thought women went for bass players."

"Bass players may get more shirts lifted their way when they're onstage, but drummers have more time to sit in the back, make eye contact, and flirt like crazy. I knew one drummer in Tulsa who swore he always went home with tens because true band groupies all know that drummers love to bang and know the best spots to hit."

It was Finn's turn to laugh. Which had him remembering that she'd made him laugh in bed, too. Which had been unusual, since he'd never really understood the need for conversation while having sex. They'd made a connection that night. In more ways than one. More ways than it was safe to think about, he reminded himself.

"Maybe I chose the wrong occupation."

"I seriously doubt you've ever had to leave a bar alone."

Because she could have been describing his early years, first in the Academy, then later as an aviator, that hit a little too close to home. There'd even been periods of overindulgence when he'd wondered if he took after his dad more than he'd thought.

Finn might not worship at the altar of dollars like Colin Brannigan had, but the old man had definitely gone through his share of women. His aunt Claire and James, who'd been old enough to remember when their mom died, said their dad had always treated Kathleen Brannigan like a queen. His aunt had even insisted that Colin hadn't always been an asshat. That he'd changed into one because his love for his wife had been so strong losing her had broken his heart in a way that had never healed.

Finn wasn't sure he believed that. But, just in case it was true, he'd decided early on that while he was willing to risk his life, there was no way he'd put his heart on the line. While he admittedly had his faults, no way did he intend to end up broken like his father.

"You weren't a pickup," he said. It was important that she understood that.

"Of course I was," she said mildly.

They were nearing Caribou, and this conversation had him feeling as if he were suddenly flying through flack like those old B-52 bombers in the World War II black-and-white flying movies he'd always loved to watch.

But there was one thing he wanted to get straight before they landed. "You were different," he said. "We were different together. Which is why you ran out. Because you felt it, too."

He found it interesting that she didn't even try to argue that point. Instead, she merely shut the conversation down by turning toward the window to watch the scenery.

5

TORI HAD BEEN to forty-nine (now fifty) states and a dozen foreign countries. Although she wasn't one to boast, she'd topped the country Billboard list in Germany for one memorable week. She'd always been popular in that country, which could have been because she sang about emotions Germans typically didn't reveal out loud. Or, she admitted, it could've been the ubiquitous steins of beer served at all the venues she'd played.

The conversation had gotten a little uncomfortable when they'd drifted into her parents' deaths. Which, in turn, had kept her from asking Finn more about his life. To do so could've caused the conversational focus to return to hers, and she wasn't prepared to share her years Carter's evil, manipulative, lying mother, who made the wicked witch of Oz look like a pussycat.

Which would then bring up why the hell she'd have even considered Carter's proposal.

Temporary insanity was her only defense. That and a ticking biological clock that had drowned out the voices of common sense trying to be heard from the back of her mind. It might not seem to outsiders to go along with the independent way she lived, but the simple fact was that she wanted a family.

She'd given up on the idea of love. But Carter hadn't offered that. His proposal had resembled a business partnership. He needed a wife to be a helpmate when he took over his father's business empire; she wanted a husband; they both wanted children. Also, he'd reminded her that there'd been a connection between them once, years ago. One that they'd never been able to test to see if it could have become serious.

Perhaps, he'd suggested slyly, once they were a couple, they could recover that. And if not, well, with fifty percent of marriages ending in divorce, what was wrong with going into a marriage with their eyes wide open?

It had all sounded so logical. Reasonable. And, as he'd said, there had been a connection. At least on her part. She'd crushed on him for years. Then, just when he'd finally noticed her...

No. Tori shook her head. That was in the past. If there was one thing she excelled at, it was never looking in the rearview mirror. She'd moved on, and yes, she was still using Carter's money, but after what he'd done, she figured she damn well deserved it. She also didn't feel guilty about taking that hundred dollars from his wallet he'd left on the dresser before he'd gone out onto the balcony to make that phone call she'd overheard.

After all, she'd paid for the white wedding dress she'd gotten from the online rental boutique where she'd found that over-the-top sequin number she'd worn the night she'd met Finn. It now occurred to her that the fact that it had been listed as "never worn" wasn't the most propitious of omens.

Although it was only going to be the two of them eloping to Vegas, she'd also snagged a bouquet from a Sunset Drive funeral home. Again, not the most positive move. However, she'd sung at enough memorial services at the funeral home's chapel that the owner had offered her some white lilies that had not only gotten yellow pollen on the dress but given her a migraine even before she'd overheard that life-changing phone call.

She'd already been feeling guilty about steal-ing the money and had been returning it to his wallet when he'd come back into the condo. And dared ask *her* what she'd been doing. Shockingly, when she'd confronted him with what she'd overheard, he hadn't even tried to deny it. But had simply pointed out, in a cool, unemotional tone, that while he regretted her learning that way, if she stopped to think about it, the idea was still a win/win for both of them. Because if she went along, she'd have enough funds to outbid whoever might try to buy her songs during the bankruptcy auction.

That was when she'd done something she'd never, ever done before. She'd slapped his smug face. When he slapped her back, although he'd never before laid a hand on her, Tori hadn't been surprised. Because she'd known, deep down, that when you supped with the devil, you needed a very long spoon.

And that's exactly what she'd been about to do.

In that way, she thought, it had all turned out for the best. Better to know the truth before taking vows to love and cherish, until death she did part, than being run down by the locomotive racing her way.

Once she'd accepted the truth, she'd moved swiftly from shocked to furious, then had already landed on optimistic about starting a new chapter in her life by the time she'd reached Anchorage.

Until she'd walked into that baggage area to find the man whom she'd tried so hard to forget, the very same one who had sent her into Carter's arms, waiting for her.

What were the odds?

Having never been that much of a gambler, Tori didn't want to think about that. Instead, she looked out the plexiglass window at the landscape that was the most magnificent she'd ever seen.

Once they'd left the slight fog of Anchorage, the air had cleared, revealing snowy mountains thrusting into a clear, robin's-egg-blue sky. A river wound its way over boulders through a mountain meadow ablaze with flowers. What looked to be goats clung to the sides of the mountains, and as he flew through a gap, she saw a herd of deer and a flash of red she thought might be a fox. But she didn't see any sign of human habitation.

"There's certainly no urban sprawl here," she murmured. What type of place had she run off to this time?

"The population density of the state is around one-point-three people per mile, which makes most of the state even less than that, since the majority live in Anchorage," he said. "I'm told lots of people get freaked out by the isolation and go back to the lower forty-eight."

"But not you," she guessed.

"I've only been here a little over a month, but after growing up in L.A. and spending so much of my naval career crowded onto a noisy, floating city that never sleeps, this feels right to me. Also, when you're out to sea, often all the scenery you get is miles of water and other ships in the fleet.

This place beats the hell out of that."

"I've never stayed in a small town more than a night."

The occasional pickup bar gigs along the way to larger venues didn't lend themselves to a sustainable income.

"Have you ever played in Texas?"

"Sure." She'd done well in Austin, Houston, Dallas, San Antonio, and Odessa down in the oil patch. Along with countless of those tiny towns between stops whose names she could no longer remember.

"Well, you're now in a state the size of Texas, California, and Montana combined. Alaska's one-fifth the size of the lower forty-eight states, but it has six hundred and forty square acres for every mile of paved roads. Which is why it also claims over a hundred seaplane bases."

"Which is good for your business."

"We're not Delta, or even Alaska, but Osprey does okay. And it's good for the people because more fly than drive to doctors or dentists or for shopping. I've got to admit, sometimes I feel kinda like St. Nick on Christmas Eve when I show up at a village with mail and packages."

"This isn't where I'd have expected you to be headed."

"It's a daily surprise to me, too," he admitted. "Which bring up the question of how you *did* think of me."

"I thought you might end up an astronaut."

"Really?" He sounded surprised. "Why?"

"Because it was obvious, from the way that commander and others with all that fruit salad on their uniforms acted around you, that you were on a fast climb up the Navy ladder. But I couldn't see you stuck in some office in the Pentagon."

"That makes two of us," he agreed.

"So, I figured the ultimate goal would be to go into space."

"Which would be way cool. But they don't go into space all that often. It's not like doing multiple missions a day. It's also a long shot because there are over four thousand applications for about twenty astronaut positions every two years."

Tori decided that it would be risky stroking his ego by stating that she didn't think the competition would be a problem.

"But even if I passed that hurdle, I'd want to be a pilot. Which sounds really appealing, but I wouldn't want that job because commanders and pilots aren't allowed to do spacewalks. Which would be the coolest thing ever."

"Why not?"

"NASA can't afford to have them stuck out-side during a possible emergency." He blew out a breath and began switching dials again. "So, I landed here."

"Where you belong?"

The grin was back. More lethal than ever. "Being California born and bred, I may wait until spring to clarify that. But meanwhile, I'm in a good place... And speaking of being in a good place, we're coming up on Caribou."

She glanced down at the town that looked like a model train set. For a very small model train. Located between a startlingly blue lake and a dark green conifer forest that rose seemingly straight up the mountains hovering over the town, it appeared to consist of a downtown area of seven streets. Three running parallel from what the plane's dashboard compass declared to be north and south, three running east and west, and one cutting kitty-corner through the center.

Most of the buildings appeared to be in toward the center of the crossroads, with the distance between the houses and cabins growing as the roads spread farther out from town. One road ended at the banks of the lake; the other appeared to run directly into the base of Mount Denali.

The town seemed to rise up as the plane lowered, allowing her to catch a glimpse of one stoplight in the center of town. It was flashing yellow.

Reminding herself that she hadn't come here

to socialize, or for a vibrant arts and music scene or active nightlight like the one she'd left behind in L.A., Tori assured herself that this was just the place to refresh and reboot.

"It looks charming," she said.

"From the air. At ground level, it's decidedly more rustic. More so the farther you get from downtown, so if you're expecting Cabot Cove, you'll be disappointed."

"You did not watch *Cabot Cove*." Next he'd be admitting to having binge-watched *Gilmore Girls*.

"I'm the wrong demographic," he confirmed. "But I've seen the village at Universal Studio's *Jaws* lake attraction. And speaking of lakes, there's a resort on this one. That's where you'll be staying."

"I thought I'd be in a cabin." It would be difficult to write her songs with people from the next-door rooms knocking on the walls and complaining about noise.

"You are. Along with the lodge, there are a dozen cabins along the lakefront. Close enough that you don't feel as if you're out all alone in the wilderness to be wolf bait or run into Sasquatch, yet far enough apart that everyone has their privacy."

"He's just a legend, right? Like the Loch Ness Monster. But furrier."

"If you stick around town long enough, you'll hear stories from locals who swear to have seen him in the wild, but my guess is they were probably smoking something funny at the time. There's also a canoe, boat rental place, and a small store. Not as well equipped as the Trading Post grocery in town, but it'll do if you're looking for 7-Eleven type stuff. Or fish bait or a chainsaw-carved moose souvenir to take home."

"I'll keep that in mind."

Not that she'd actually buy such a thing even if she *had* a home. But before leaving town, she'd arranged with a moving company to pick up all her stuff and put it in storage, and told her best friend and roommate—Zoe Long, a bass player for an all-girl band called Pandora's Box—to go ahead and find someone to take her bedroom in their rented '30s Spanish-style bungalow. Thanks to the influx of more and more indie musicians and hipsters who'd been finding Echo Park after being priced out of other neighborhoods undergoing gentrification, she suspected her eight-by-ten-foot room had probably been snatched off Craigslist before her plane had taken off from LAX.

Not that she intended to go back. While Tori wasn't sure what she was going to do once the two weeks' rent on the cabin ran out, she did know that she'd be moving on. Because that's what she'd been doing for more than half her life. And while it might not be what, in a perfect world, she would have chosen, she knew, more than most, that perfection was a myth perpetuated by those control freaks who needed to believe it possible.

6

HAVING GROWN UP flying before he'd been old enough to get his driver's learning permit, and later landing on carriers, when he'd first arrived in Caribou, even knowing its reputation from his trip with his dad years ago, Finn had secretly scoffed at the bulky, cumbersome-looking Beaver with those fat pontoons hanging down like torpedoes. The best planes had jets, and all real planes had wheels.

Despite being unimpressed, by the end of his second week, given all the inlets, lakes, and rivers, he'd come to realize that the floatplane was as ubiquitous a way to travel as the dog sled had been in an earlier era. Which was when one of the senior pilots, Jackie Johnson—nicknamed "Mother Goose" because she'd grown up flying with her dad in his twin-engine Grumman Goose amphibian around the Aleutian—told him that if he was going to take bush flying seriously and rid himself of his *cheechako* a.k.a. newcomer, label, he was going to have to man up and learn how to fly the Beaver. Or find himself another airline to work for.

Since no one knew he owned Osprey Air, losing his job wasn't a problem. But Finn had never been one to back away from a challenge. If this sixty-something native Alaskan thought he wasn't pilot enough to manage a floatplane, then he was damn well going to show her how badly she'd underestimated him.

What he'd underestimated was that flying a floatplane wasn't like any other. Taking off and landing was entirely different, given that he was piloting a boat rather than a plane when he was in the water.

Not laughing at him, at least too badly, every time he screwed up, Jackie had taught him that, contrary to instinct, a glassy lake was the most difficult surface to land on and caused the most floatplane accidents because without some disturbance on the water, there was no way to calculate depth.

So, he'd spent hours practicing reading the water for wind direction, learning how to calculate the curvature of the waves the way he'd once prepared for the deck tail hook. He'd learned that waves creating visible foam as they broke on waves indicated too much sea swell for a safe beaching. She'd taught him to circle before landing to scout for potentially deadly rocks and driftwood, and how to land parallel to swells to avoid skipping like the rocks he and his brothers used to skip across the pond at the ranch.

Just like when he'd attended Topgun school, he'd discovered how much he still had to learn. And that he could probably spend the rest of his life studying and practicing and still screw things up.

Which he had no intention of doing today.

Manipulating the throttle, rudder, ailerons, and flaps, he set the plane down onto the lake, then, using the drift, sailed the plane backwards, avoiding boats, docked floatplanes, and pilings on which seagulls perched, waiting for his wake to stir up any food, and ran up onto the designated plank.

Then cut the engine. And began breathing again.

"Okay," she said. "I'm duly impressed."

"Just doing my job." He'd heard that several times a day from tourists since he'd started flying on the summer schedule, but this time was different. Her compliment shouldn't mean so much. But it did.

"That may be. But it was like watching a composer both conduct and play. Like a one-man orchestra," she said. "I'm beginning to see why switching careers hasn't been a problem for you.

That's got to be as much of a challenge as landing on a carrier."

"It doesn't have as much potential for disaster, but it's always interesting," he agreed. "One of the reasons I left when I did was that the Navy was starting to bring in an auto system called the MAGIC CARPET."

"You're kidding, right?"

"No. Like all government agencies, the military loves its acronyms. This one stands for *Maritime Augmented Guidance with Integrated Controls for Carrier Approach and Recovery Precision Enabling Technologies.*"

"I wonder how long it took to come up with that."

"There are probably programs. Like when you go online and choose your Star Wars commander name," he said. "And it makes sense because when you're landing on a carrier, you need to maintain a three-degree glide slope while staying lined up with a moving ship and keeping the jet's nose at just the right angle so it doesn't slam into the deck.

"That can take three hundred different adjustments with the stick and throttle—left and right, back and forth to put the nose up or down, constant acceleration and deceleration with the throttle to make up for any power lost with all that moving around—all in just eighteen seconds before hitting the deck and snagging the tail hook perfectly across one of the four wires."

"Wow." Her eyes widened. "I knew it was dangerous. And yes, I got that from watching *Top Gun* and *NCIS*, but I never realized it was that scary."

"That's the rush," he admitted. "The stress level is off the charts, especially when you're not just talking about the possibility of killing yourself and costing the Navy a bunch of money, but there are also all the LSOs and other ground crew on the deck who can die if you screw up.

"The system puts a jet into an automatic landing mode that guides its trajectory to the deck. Basically, you just take the stick and push it forward until you're on the glide slope, let go, and keep your hands off."

"And here I'm not sure I'm ready to hand over control to a self-driving car," she said.

"I talked with a pilot who tested it and found he was uncomfortable with how few inputs he was making," Finn allowed.

"That's because you're all control freaks," she said without any hint of accusation. It was merely an observation he couldn't deny.

"I know a lot of pilots who are afraid it'll take away the badass aspect. The hey-I'm-cool-because-I'm-a-carrier-aviator part."

"Which is admittedly way cool," she allowed.

"True. And I'm not going to deny that was always part of the appeal since I was a kid. But landings are not only like jumping out of a tenth-story window and trying to hit a postage stamp with your tongue. In reality, they're just what you've got to do after you've completed a mission. So, it makes sense, if it can be done more safely by computerization, then hooyah for technology."

"You said that was *one* of your reasons for leaving the Navy," she said, making him realize he'd screwed up and opened the conversation to a place he wasn't prepared to go. "What were the others?"

"Different things," he said offhandedly. No way did he want to admit that having nearly died twice, he decided against going for the hat trick of death escapes. "Including this opportunity showing up. Want to stop by the Caribou Café on the way to your cabin, get some lunch, and you can tell me all the reasons you bailed on your wedding?" A thought belatedly occurred to him. "You did leave before getting to the 'I do' part, right?"

"Fortunately. And thanks for the offer of lunch, but I ate on the plane. It's been a long day and I'd just as soon get settled into the cabin."

And not talk about her botched nuptials. Got it.

"Works for me," he said agreeably. It was just

as well. If they got into the wedding, they'd get into Covington IV, which would put him in a situation where he'd either have to admit he knew the guy, which would open up a lot of questions Finn wasn't prepared to answer, or pretend to have never heard of him.

So, he'd drop her off at the cabin without mentioning that not only had his deceased father built the resort but that it continued to earn money for his estate. The place was being locally managed by Barbara Ann Carter and handled by an army of lawyers for the next five years. It wasn't like Tori needed to know that. The same way there was no reason for her to think he was anything but merely an employee of Osprey Air.

That's a great many sins of omission you're committing, Finn Brannigan, he heard Sister Bartholomew's stern voice from the back of his mind.

No offense intended, Sister, Finn shot back. *But please shut the hell up. I know what I'm doing.*

Which was yet another lie. This one Finn knew he was telling to himself.

TORI WAS SURPRISED when she discovered that Finn had landed the plane at the resort. "Doesn't the town have an actual airport?" she asked.

"Sure. But it's on the other side of the lake,

next to the town's gravel runway for wheeled planes. But you said you wanted to get settled, so this is quicker."

"That's very personal service."

He shrugged. "Osprey isn't a big airline. We like to think that while we may not serve meals, except for when passengers order bag lunches from the café for a day of sightseeing, we raise the bar for personalized service."

"I can't argue that." She found getting out of the plane a little easier than getting in and decided that perhaps that was because she was no longer scared spitless.

"Your cabin's down the road a bit," he said after tying down the Beaver and retrieving her suitcase. Then, just as he had in the terminal, he put his hand on the small of her back and led her to a gleaming red Jeep Grand Cherokee with a white Osprey Air logo on the side. "Although it's a short walk, given your stuff, I'll drive you up there."

"At least if you get lost in the mountains, you won't be hard to spot from the air."

While painted the same fire-engine red as the Corvette she'd seen him leave with the hotel valet, it was definitely not built for speed. Since valet service hadn't been included in the gig, she'd parked her five-year-old Corolla—which she'd bought when she'd signed that record contract that was now in limbo—in the self-park lot. He hadn't noticed her at the time. But her attention had definitely been drawn to him, even if he hadn't been wearing his whites. It also hadn't escaped her attention that the young woman valet had been on the verge of swooning at his feet as he'd handed over the keys.

"You laugh," he said easily, thankfully unaware of her thoughts, "but it's true. I've done enough search and rescue to know that a white vehicle is not the best idea up here after Labor Day." He opened the back. "You can put your guitar in here. I'll drive you to the cabin."

"Which reminds me," she said, wondering why she or Carter hadn't thought of it, "I'm going to need to rent a car. Does this town even have a Hertz franchise?"

"Nope, but it's not a problem," he assured her. "There's a B and B only five miles away that rents cars. We work with them a lot during the season, but not enough that it makes it financially worthwhile to get into business ourselves."

"I'm not taking your SUV. Which is way more car than I'll be needing. I'd feel as if I were driving a tank."

"Fine. I'll bring a smaller ride out to you in the morning and we can switch."

She paused before climbing up into the Jeep's passenger seat, which seemed nearly as high as the one in the floatplane. "Surely you don't treat every passenger to this much personal service."

"No. When I saw you come into the baggage claim area alone, I figured something had happened, so I called the office, and Mary Muldoon—who opened Osprey with her husband, who passed on a few years ago—called the car rental place to check. Seems your former fiancé cancelled the car while you were in the air and I was on the way to Anchorage. So Mary had two of the guys deliver my rig out here."

"Why?"

"Because whatever happened, it couldn't have been your best day."

His mild tone suggested that it wasn't any big deal. But it was. It wasn't as if they'd made any promises that night. In fact, it had been just the opposite. He'd told her straight out that he wasn't into relationships, and she'd assured him back that she hadn't been looking for one.

Still, if they'd ended up in her room instead of his suite, and he'd been the one to sneak out without a word, she'd have been hurt. Maybe even angry. Which he'd undoubtedly been, yet here he was, going the extra effort to make her feel better.

Which, conversely, only made her feel worse. Especially since she hadn't been able to stop thinking about him since that night.

"It hasn't been one of my best days," she said, deciding to outwardly treat it as casually as he seemed to. "So, thank you."

He shrugged. "No problem. So, let's go."

THE CABIN WASN'T nearly as rustic as she'd been expecting, given the size of the town she'd seen from the air. The outside was made of long yellow logs Finn told her were native white spruce. What appeared to be red shingles on the roof were actually made of metal.

"It doesn't look like the corrugated metal I've seen on barns," she said.

"That's because the owner didn't want guests to feel like they were staying in a barn," he said. "These hold up to our weather a lot better over time and drive down energy costs. Metal reflects heat, creating a barrier that blocks the sun's summer heat. In the winter, the reflective properties keep heat in. Plus, it's recyclable."

"I'm all for energy conservation, but I doubt I'll be here when winter arrives."

"Which is usually September. Or earlier. And I thought your plans were fluid."

"They are." She sighed and decided there was no shame in her situation. It wasn't as if she'd done anything wrong. "My bank account is less so. I plan to take advantage of all this gorgeous scenery to write some new songs, then go back to the States—"

"This *is* a state," Finn reminded her.

"Yes. Of course." She suspected he heard that a lot. But the truth was, from what she'd seen the short time since flying into Anchorage, Alaska seemed very foreign. In a vast, amazing way. "But I doubt it has much of a music scene."

From all that empty space and lack of roads she'd seen from the air, she imagined a touring singer could spend more time traveling from venue to venue than performing.

"The Gold Gulch Saloon and Dance Hall, which is attached to the Caribou Café, has bands, especially during the summer for the tourist season. Barbara Ann was complaining last week that she'd lost one of the bands she'd been counting on staying through the summer to a resort down in Washington state. If you're looking for a pickup gig, she'd probably scoop you up like white on rice."

She tilted her head and looked up at him. "That's quite a Southern expression for a SoCal guy. You did grow up in California, right?"

"Barbara Ann's Southern with one of those larger-than-life personalities that tends to rub off on you. And yeah, I grew up in Calabasas."

Her eyes narrowed as her shoulders stiffened. "That's a pricey area."

"Pricey being relative."

"I played a political fund-raiser there at some movie mogul's mansion. It looked as if it had been designed by Marie Antoinette and was packed with one-percenters dressed for a red-carpet event. The bling was blinding, and the perfume and designer male colognes practically shut down my lungs."

"That sure as hell wouldn't have been our place." He grinned. "Can you see seven raucous boys living in a California version of Versailles very long without destroying the place? We were a lot more rural. Mostly we ran wild in the mountains and fished in a small pond on the property. We did have a pool," he allowed. "I hope you're not going to hold that against me."

"Of course not."

His explanation made more sense. Despite having had a career that put him in a very small fraternity, Finn Brannigan seemed like a regular guy. Tori couldn't imagine him living in a house like the Covington estate where her parents had worked impossibly long hours for what she later came to realize was peon wages.

By the time she'd died, Tori's mother had advanced to delegating contracted hourly staff rather than cleaning the ten toilets herself. Keeping all the schedules straight and making certain that everyone was working up to Helen

Covington's impossible-to-please standards was akin to juggling flaming torches while walking a tightrope, but Tori had always thought her mother probably could have planned the D-day invasion while whipping up a formal dinner for eight.

Which brought back a memory of standing on a box to reach the counter while her mother taught her to make a *soufflé au fromage*. Although seemingly simple, the dish offered many opportunities for disaster. But her mother didn't seem intimidated as she quoted Audrey Hepburn's culinary chef from *Sabrina*: "It must be like two butterflies dancing the waltz in the summer breeze," Anna Cassidy had said gaily, fluttering her hands over the pan after pouring the cheese and egg mixture into the dish, as if performing a magic trick.

Which she had. At the end of the cooking time, nothing less than a masterpiece had come from the oven.

The memory, like so many others of life with her parents, was bittersweet. She remembered the pleasure of her mother singing as she whisked the mixture with a skill Tori, who considered herself a pretty good home cook, had never been able to master.

She'd been allowed to taste the backup just-in-case version, and while the bottom and sides had crusted together to form an exquisitely thick cheese layer, the inside had been like eating a cloud.

Thinking back on Finn's question about the afterlife, Tori decided that if there was a heaven, her mother's cheese soufflé would be the starter for every party.

Tori had bussed the dinner table that night and remembered Helen Covington offering not a single word of praise for what had, indeed, been culinary magic.

But her mind had wandered off track again. As it seemed to have been doing the past year. Ever since her reckless night with Finn.

Tori was not impulsive by nature. Her life, after her parents' deaths, had been so unstable that, while she might not have chosen a practical, stable occupation like accounting or teaching, until that mess with her recording contract, she'd managed to take care of herself.

The luck of where she'd been born had helped a great deal. California was one of the better states for supporting fosters once they reached the age to leave the system. Some merely said, "Good-bye and good luck" once you hit eighteen. But she'd had counselors who helped with housing subsidies when she applied for early emancipation once she'd graduated high school a week after her seventeenth birthday.

Then others who'd helped her apply for a Pell Grant and cobble together scholarships. Using those, along with working as a line cook in a West Hollywood pub and tips from singing at various local events, she'd been able to earn an associate arts degree in music from Los Angeles City College.

She'd considered transferring to UCLA, but by the time her two years at LACC were coming to an end, she'd just wanted to get out and start getting on with real-life. That had been ten years ago, and although there'd been some very lean times, and her financial situation was admittedly in a mess right now, she had her music, her Taylor, and, as her parents always liked to say, her health.

This was not the end of the road. Merely a detour, and if there was one thing Tori had become accustomed to, it was all the various twists and turns life could take. For now, she'd enjoy the view of this dazzling, impossibly blue lake and the mountains that towered over Caribou, refill her creative well, write some new songs, then come up with a revised plan to get on with her life.

7

THE CABIN HAD two front doors with a few feet of space in between, which Finn told her kept mud and snow from being tracked into the house along with keeping the winter cold out and the inside heat from escaping.

She stopped so quickly in the doorway leading into the central, open space, that Finn nearly ran into her. Since the top of her head only came up to his shoulders, he had no trouble seeing past her to a scene that looked straight out of a *Bridezillas* episode. A show which, although Finn had always viewed it as yet another reason never to get married, one of the pilots on the *O'Halloran* had downloaded onto his computer. When asked why anyone would waste valuable rack time on so much over-the-top female drama, the guy, who'd recently gotten engaged, had claimed to be war-gaming his upcoming wedding.

"Oh, wow." She stared up at the huge banner of honeycomb paper balls in varying shades of pink and white that hung over a white-draped table on which a bottle of pink champagne on ice and two flutes rimmed in gold sat.

Clear balloons filled with pastel and gold confetti were floating high above the room, all the way to the top of the cathedral ceiling. A tiered three-layer cake featuring a mountain scene airbrushed on the side in purple and blues and some kind of sugary trees and a marzipan bride and groom in hiking gear standing on top claimed the center of the table, while yet more confetti, along with gold and pink glitter, was scattered over the cloth.

Someone had written on a chalkboard standing next to the table, *Old, New, Borrowed, and Blue. Tori and Carter have said, I DO!*

Hell. As soon as he'd realized what happened, he should've known to call Barbara Ann, just in case she had something like this in mind. *Just in case?* How could she not? The woman might have lived in Caribou for most of her adult life, having come here as a teenage bride, but except for a mind for business he suspected could match any of those hedge fund guys making billions on Wall Street, Barbara Ann Carter was Southern to the bone. No way would she not pull out all the decorating stops for a honeymoon.

"I'm sorry. Like I said, the woman who manages the resort is from the South," he said by way of explanation. "While most people around here tend to be pretty casual, when it comes to anything festive, Barbara Ann goes full steam ahead."

"I played with a band for a short time in Savannah and attended a wedding shower for the female bass player." Her gaze drifted up to the ceiling where the balloons had gathered. "This is actually low-key compared to that."

There was a note in a gilt envelope on the table. Tori opened it and read the few lines out loud. "Welcome, Lovebirds! Wishing you the best, most romantic honeymoon ever, and if there's anything you need, just dial the desk from the phone and we'll send it right over…

"Meanwhile, in case you'd rather eat in, at least for your first few days (wink, wink), the fridge and pantry are stocked with basics, and I've put some of the café's most popular meals in the freezer. We're all so delighted you've come to visit us! Hugs and all best wishes, Barbara Ann Carter, resort manager and mayor of Caribou." She slipped the note back into the envelope. "That's very thoughtful. And sweet."

"Like I said, she's Southern." To use one of Barbara Ann's own expressions, the woman might be as sweet as pecan pie, but she was also a force of nature. Which, he figured, was how she'd managed to fit into a place which originally had to have seemed as alien to her as Mars.

"I can get rid of these decorations for you."

Finn couldn't remember ever seeing so much pink in one place. He might be risking estrogen poisoning without first putting on a hazmat suit, but the last thing Tori needed was a reminder of whatever had caused her to end up at her Alaskan honeymoon cabin without a groom.

"No." She glanced down at the floor, where pink silk rose petals had been scattered in a trail formation. "It's okay." She dragged a hand down her face, which was beginning to show her fatigue. The blue smudges beneath her eyes were now at risk for having the airlines tag them as excess luggage. "I have a feeling those lead to the bedroom."

"Yeah. They probably do." Caribou's mayor was a wonderful woman. No one ever entered the café or her mayor's office without receiving a warm, welcoming hug. But subtlety wasn't exactly her forte. "There's probably a broom somewhere to sweep it up."

Finn glanced around. Where did people keep brooms, anyway? When he wasn't living on a carrier, where there was a place for everything and everything had its place, he tended toward hotel apartments that came with housekeeping. And the first thing he did when he'd landed in town nearly a month ago had been to hire a woman to come in once a week to clean the house he'd found also came with the airline as the official CEO residence.

As far as anyone but Mary Muldoon knew, he was renting it for the summer. Although he'd received a few comments about how he could afford the place at high tourist season, his story about having saved up some dough during all the years in the Navy seemed to have been accepted.

She held up a hand. "It's okay. Really. I'll get to it later. After I shower off the travel grime. And maybe take a nap."

"Let me at least carry your bag into the master suite."

Where she'd be staying alone. Knowing Carter, he suspected the guy had done something douchey to have her calling off the wedding. Then again, Carter George Covington IV had never realized the value of anything or anyone, so he could have been stupid enough to let Tori Cassidy get away.

Hello, pot. This is kettle. Calling you black.

As they'd suspected, the damn petals led to a king-sized bed crafted from local logs that looked out the French doors leading to the secluded deck to the forest and Denali beyond. Unfortunately, the bed's blue coverlet had been covered with yet more petals, and candles seemed to have been placed on every flat surface. Including, he could see as he glanced into the bathroom, around the edge of a Jacuzzi tub large enough to do laps in.

"Well, whoever designed this definitely wasn't a minimalist," she murmured, seeming a bit stunned.

"The tub's probably for the winter crowd," he said, holding back the information that his father had been the one to push the architect for what he'd dubbed *rustic opulence*. "I'm told a lot of Osprey's winter flying is taking groups up on the mountain for skiing and snowboarding."

"Wow." She looked out the window, a long, long way up the mountain. "You're going to be landing up there?"

"So they say."

"Have you ever done that?"

"No. But the SEALs do extreme winter training in Washington's Olympic Mountains. I've flown teams onto glaciers there, so it should be pretty much the same thing."

She shook her head. "That's just crazy."

"Different strokes."

She'd given him that head tilt again and was studying him as if seeing him for the first time. She wasn't alone. Now that he thought about it, he couldn't deny that it sounded not entirely sane. But hey, someone had to do it. And as far as he was concerned, although the other services would probably disagree, there weren't any pilots better than the ones found in the Navy.

"You really don't miss the Navy?"

"Nope."

He missed the comradery, the sense of family the Navy had provided, more so, honestly, than he'd gotten from his own. But there was an old saying that there were old pilots and bold pilots, but there were no old, bold pilots. At twenty-seven he wasn't even nearing old, but having escaped death twice had left Finn fearing that he was coming close to losing his edge.

Maybe, as Mary had suggested when he'd first shown up at Osprey's offices, he hadn't lost his edge at all but was merely growing up. Which was another thing he'd think about during those hours flying the blue and orange bags of mail and crates of supplies through the mountains and valleys.

"I'd miss singing," she volunteered after he'd placed her bag on the wooden luggage rack by the closet. "But fortunately, it doesn't involve risking my life."

Deciding not to mention all the singers who'd died in plane crashes, Finn didn't respond to that statement. "You all set?" he asked instead.

"Yes, thank you." She was walking him back down the rose-petal trail when she paused at the table.

"You sure you don't want me to at least take the cake?" he asked. The other pilots would scarf it down like a bear preparing for winter hibernation.

"It's fine. Someone went to a lot of trouble to create it. I'd hate the word to get around town that I didn't appreciate it."

"I guess you might have appreciated it more if the situation had been different."

Her laughter had lost its music. "Now that you put it that way, I'm going to take all this"— she waved her arms at the cake, the confetti, glitter, the floating balloons, and Pepto-Bismol puffy pink garland—"as a reward. For avoiding the worst mistake of my life."

"Good plan." It wasn't entirely a full explanation about what had happened, but at least she didn't seem on the verge of bursting into tears. Which was a relief. Finn would rather face down a horde of armed terrorists than a woman's tears. "I'm told positivity is always a plus. Plus, it annoys enough people to be worth the effort."

"I'll keep that in mind." Her lips twitched in what appeared to be a true attempt at a smile, and a bit of the light returned to her eyes.

Because he wanted to stay, Finn reminded himself that he had a full schedule today. And, although he hadn't asked for it, still wasn't sure he *wanted* it, he did have an airline to run.

But that didn't mean that, when he stood in the doorway, looking down at that exhausted but still lovely face, he didn't feel something move inside him. And not just in the obvious parts that had responded to her from the beginning but in an unfamiliar place that had him rubbing his chest over his heart.

8

NOT WANTING TO be too obvious, rather than go out on the front porch, Tori stood in front of the front room window, watching him head down the road to where he'd docked the floatplane. She was emotionally drained, exhausted, and she knew that once she got some sleep, she'd be back to being angry as hell, but right now, she allowed herself to watch his butt in those perfectly fitting jeans as he walked away.

It really was a great butt, she thought with a wistful sigh. Correction. Make that an excellent butt. And, as if they had a mind of their own, her palms suddenly remembered cupping those well-muscled glutes. Which, while perking up other parts of her body, had her feeling even more depressed.

You could have had him. Not forever. Maybe no more than another day. She vaguely remembered him mentioning something about going sailing. But her brain had been so sex-fogged, he might have merely been saying it was something he'd like to do. It could have had nothing to do with her.

Except…

For those hours they'd spent together, he'd proven totally focused on her. At least on her body, finding erogenous zones she hadn't even realized she possessed, and then once discovered, he'd set them off. Again. And again. And again.

Damn. She so didn't need this trip down memory lane.

Shaking her hands and shoulders, she took a deep breath, found her center and went back down the pink-petal hallway into the bathroom, and, skipping the hedonistic tub, opted for the walk-in shower.

Although all the candles and the petals were definitely overkill, and she wasn't going to have any use for the warming eatable massage lotion, chocolate play crayons, or the—heaven help her—male erection enhancement gel, Tori did bless Barbara Ann Carter, wherever she was, for the fabulous collection of shampoo, body soap, and lotion.

Changing into a pair of pajamas she'd thrown into her bag after tossing out some overpriced, highly uncomfortable honeymoon lingerie, she pulled back the comforter and tumbled into bed.

And discovered that it was possible to be too

exhausted to fall asleep.

She got out of bed and closed the blackout drapes, blocking both the sun and stimulating view. She lay back down, snuggled into the puffy down pillows, took a deep breath, held it, and slowly let it out. Just like the meditation she did every day before writing.

Breathe. Hold. Exhale.

Breathe. Hold. Exhale.

Repeat.

And still, her mind whirled, rerunning the events of the past twenty-four hours in high definition with an amplified theater sound system.

She thought of all the things she'd said when she'd confronted her lying, cheating, playboy fiancé. Which had her thinking of all the things she wished she'd said. Things she still wanted to say. Not wanting to show weakness, except for that slap, she'd stayed outwardly cool. Calm. While inside she'd been screeching like a banshee and throwing things at Carter George Covington IV's head.

No, better yet, she'd had a fantasy flash of marching into the kitchen that his hired personal chef had stocked with more utensils than any Iron Chef probably owned, finding the biggest, sharpest, most badass carving knife, and Bobbitizing the son of a bitch. After which she'd throw his cheating penis and his balls into the sea outside the deck in hopes a hungry killer shark came swimming by.

That's what she'd wanted to do. That's how the drama that had kept running in an endless loop in her mind all during her trip up here to Alaska should have ended.

Strangely, the voices had quieted in her head while she'd been flying with Finn. But only because they'd been replaced by other, equally stimulating memories.

Now, as she lay in the king-sized bed, which, thankfully, at least wasn't clichéd honeymoon round, smelling like a woman who'd prepared to be well and expertly laid, she found both her engagement and her night with Finn playing in her mind.

Neither of them had ended well.

Just like everything else in her life.

Which, in turn, had her whirling, buzzing mind going back to Finn's question about the afterlife. What if those people who believed in reincarnation were right? What if all her problems were karma for past sins? Given the events of the past few months, if that were true, she must have been a terrible person in some past life.

Not wanting to dwell on that idea, she closed her eyes tight and took another deep breath. Which only had her realizing that she might have made a mistake going so heavy on that vanilla and almond scented body lotion which had her suddenly craving sweets. And, as it happened, just down that rose-petal hall, there was a blue and white mountain of a cake that wasn't going to eat itself.

✧   ✧   ✧

FINN THOUGHT ABOUT her all day. Which wasn't that big a surprise since he'd thought about her too much over the past months. Believing you were about to die had a guy, even one who'd never been all that introspective, thinking about regrets.

Not that Finn had all that many, at least ones he could have changed. It wasn't as if life was like *Quantum Leap*, where he could jump back in time like Scott Bakula and stop that teenage kid who'd killed his mother from getting his driver's license, which would have kept him from being on the same road she'd been that night she'd gone out for ice cream to bring back to the family.

But he was human and prone to mistakes. Including the one that hadn't stopped gnawing at him. Letting Tori Cassidy walk out of that suite at the Del.

Maybe he'd been given a do-over, he considered, as he flew a family of five over the mountains, swooping down near the five-hundred-foot FAA ceiling limit to give them an up-close view of a herd of about a hundred caribou, which was rare, since those animals tended to stick together in groups of half a dozen or less.

He'd been told that where you saw caribou, you tended to spot grizzlies, who preyed on them. His first day at Osprey, Yazz had told him about a time he'd gone low to show off a pack of wolves. Which had gotten everyone really excited, and boded well for a big tip, until he'd gotten close enough for his passengers to witness the pack tearing apart a downed deer, which, in turn, had resulted in a six-year-old girl bawling her pretty little blue eyes out about Bambi all the way back to the airport.

Not wanting to risk any *Wild Kingdom* drama today, Finn continued on, following the river back to the airfield.

"Unless you've got a last-minute booking, I think I'll take off," he told Mary after handing her the passengers' performance survey cards and putting his tip in the coffee fund jar.

Finn always felt strange pocketing the tips tourists and even some locals gave him, but he couldn't exactly explain that he didn't need it, and even more, as the owner of Osprey Air, wasn't entitled. He made his living by the company doing well. Which, thanks to his father's investment several years ago, (which he'd only found out about when he'd inherited the airline), Mary's expert management skills, and a crew of excellent, extroverted pilots, it was going gangbusters. Enough that he'd really have to go out of his way to screw it up badly enough to lose money.

"Taking the Subaru out to the runaway bride?" she asked as she flipped through the review cards.

"Barbara Ann did a good job of stocking the place, but she might like to come into town. Maybe go shopping."

"Good plan. She probably couldn't find herself one of those nifty souvenir moose antler hats back home on Rodeo Drive."

"Or a mountain wedding cake." Mary and Barbara Ann were thick as thieves. It would've been surprising for her not to have known about the decorating.

"I didn't find out about that until it was too late," she defended herself. "Barbara Ann wanted to keep it a surprise."

"It was that," he allowed.

She cringed. "Was it too terrible? Did she cry?"

"I think she was too stunned. But she handled it well and just said something about taking a shower and climbing into bed."

Which had also been something he'd been thinking about too much today. When he'd found his mind wandering to a naked Tori Cassidy beneath that rain-shower spray, spreading bubbles on a body he could remember in his sleep, he'd lowered the steel gates in his mind and forced his attention on his job. The plane might be different, the Alaska Range the total opposite of a flattop, but the fact remained that a lack of attention could result in death. Not just his own but his passengers'.

"I figured I'd have a couple of the mechanics take the car over there in the morning," she said.

"I don't mind. And it's not out of the way." Another thing he hadn't mentioned to Tori was that he lived on a cove not that far from the resort.

"Funny. For a pilot who'd rather fly mail than tourists, seems you're suddenly keen on talking with this one."

He shrugged and met that steady, knowing gaze that told him she could see right through him. "She's had a bad day. And it's not that far."

"And she's probably emotionally fragile right now."

Okay. That warning came out of left field. He'd expected her to be up to some matchmaking. Ever since he'd arrived in Caribou, she'd offered to set him up with various women. Including one of her many nieces. And she wasn't the only one. Barbara Ann appeared to have made it her personal mission to hook him up with someone.

"Is she pretty?"

There was no point in lying. "Yeah. She is." Which didn't begin to cover those glossy curls and dark eyes, but not being totally brain-dead, Finn didn't give her even more encouragement by elaborating.

"I Googled her. She's beyond pretty. As Barbara Ann would say, the girl's a picture. Which means that as soon as she makes it into town, all the males in the valley are going to take notice quicker than a well digger's ass." Mary had many sterling qualities, but her language skills tended to slide into malapropisms that everyone in town seemed to take for granted.

"So," she decided, putting the stack of cards away in her top drawer, "it's good that you're going to take advantage of the pole position. Get up there in first place."

9

FINN HAD INTENDED to simply switch cars and avoid waking Tori up since she'd probably crashed soon after he'd left. But as he pulled up in front of the house, he saw her move across the window. And despite the sun still being up after ten, it appeared she had every light in the place turned on. He also heard music coming from the high-tech sound system installed into all the rentals.

Huh.

The sun didn't set until 11:53 tonight. And the weather was scheduled to stay clear. Maybe he'd take her up to share the mountain's alpenglow. It wasn't that he intended to hit on her, although Mary's comment about all the other guys in town who'd be after her had continued to ring in his ears all the way around the lake from the airfield to here.

His job was to show tourists his adopted state. And, although he was off the clock, Finn couldn't think of a better introduction to this land of the midnight sun that had already begun to feel more like home than California had been once the last of his brothers had left the ranch.

The music was loud enough that he had to knock three times before she opened the door. Her hair was a wild cloud of dark curls around her head, tumbling over her shoulders, and even without makeup, she was stunning. She was wearing a pair of pajama shorts printed with penguins and a white cotton tank that showed off a California tan. She was also holding a half-empty glass of champagne.

Alarm sirens blaring, he was prepared to tell her that he'd brought her car and take off, when she reached across the open doorway, grabbed him by the front of his T-shirt, and tugged him into the room.

"You're just in time," she said. "I was getting lonely. It's no fun celebrating alone."

"Why are we celebrating?" Damn. Her free hand shouldn't feel so good splayed across his chest.

"Freedom." Swaying either to the music or because she was no longer capable of standing upright, she trailed a fingernail down his shirt. He couldn't decide if he was glad or not when she stopped just as that nail—the color of the coral he'd seen while scuba diving on Maui—clicked on his metal belt buckle. "And this wild gypsy rover escaping marriage captivity."

If there was one thing Finn didn't want to think about, it was how wild this gypsy rover could be. And that had been without nearly a bottle of champagne. She'd said that night that she didn't tend to drink much because liquor went straight to her head. She hadn't exaggerated. The woman was well on the way to being wasted. But, damn it, still too appealing for comfort.

"Sounds good to me," he said. Finn had seen others, including, this past year, all his brothers, who appeared to find marriage to be a great institution. He'd just never been able to imagine spending his life in an institution.

"And, for the record, this is definitely *not* a pity party," she said.

"That's good to know." He skimmed a look over her. "I like the outfit."

She glanced down at herself, as if surprised to see the penguins on her thighs. "This wasn't what I'd planned to be wearing my honeymoon night."

He had to bite his tongue to keep from saying that if he'd been Dickhead Carter George Covington IV, she wouldn't have had to worry about what to wear on her honeymoon night, because he'd have had her naked as soon as he'd gotten her in the door.

"I rented my dress, because I figured I

wouldn't be wearing it again, and got a good deal on my flowers, but for some reason I went crazy and nearly maxed out my credit card at Victoria's Secret," she said. "I went all white, not because I'm a virgin, which I'm not, as, well, of course you know…"

Finn did, all too well. And didn't really need a reminder while he was picturing her in anything from the Victoria's Secret catalog that proved nearly as popular aboard the boat as the *Sports Illustrated* swimsuit issue.

"Anyway, it turns out that white doesn't have to look virginal anymore. I left the Hollywood Boulevard store with this white see-though baby-doll nightie with a lace halter top"—she covered one breast with her hand, making him all too aware that she wasn't wearing a bra beneath that camisole—"and a lace thong. Oh, and the saleswoman talked me into a lace white garter belt."

His gaze followed her hand as it slid down her side, over the indentation at her waist, the curve of her hips, to mid-thigh. "That attached to a pair of lace-topped white nylons."

Why didn't she just kill him now?

"You need a drink," she said.

He was just blessing her change of subject when, oh, hell, she curved her fingers around the denim waistband of his jeans and began tugging

him across the floor toward the table. Not only
had she made serious inroads on the mountain
cake, the level of champagne in the green bottle
was below the halfway point. Which explained
why she was swaying a lot like a willow in a
typhoon.

"Thanks, but I'd better pass," he said. Not
only had champagne always tasted like carbonated
piss to him, the last thing this situation needed
was more alcohol. "I've got an early flight
tomorrow."

"I suppose it's just as well." She gave him a
wide, wobbly smile as she picked up the bottle,
topped off her glass, and drank like a longshore-
man tossing back a shot of whiskey. "That leaves
all the more for me." Her eyes were nearly as
glazed as the brilliantly glaciated lake he'd landed
the floatplane on earlier, before he'd left.

Then—*oh, hell*—she twined her arms around
his neck. "Dance with me."

The only reason he was putting his hands on
her hips was to steady her, Finn assured himself as
she began humming along with the lyrics coming
from the hidden speakers.

"I want a man who knows what I am," she
sang.

She was pressed against him, breasts against
his chest, belly to belly, thigh to thigh, and those
really dangerous parts in between.

"At ease, Sailor," she chided as he stiffened his shoulders and tried to put some space between them, which was difficult when she was twined around him like poison ivy.

Not that he'd normally complain, but while he might not have inherited a monogamy gene, he'd totally bought into the officer-and-a-gentleman behavior that had been drilled into him at the Academy. The Navy's reputation for a girl in every port undoubtedly went back to the Phoenicians, and Finn wasn't about to deny that there'd been times, when he'd been younger, when he'd lived up to that reputation. But he'd still always had some set-in-concrete rules of behavior.

At the top of that list was never, *ever* go to bed with a woman, no matter how seemingly willing or eager, who'd slid beyond slightly tipsy to flat-out drunk.

"Find me," she sang along with the clear so-prano voice, going up on her toes to nuzzle his neck. "Find me." She nipped at his earlobe, crooning into his ear. "Find me."

And then, her mouth found his, rocking him to the core while stealing the breath from his lungs.

She tasted of buttercream, sex, and too much temptation. When her tongue glided silkily against his, Finn heard a moan, not sure whether it had come from him or her. But it didn't matter because he had no business letting things get this far.

"Sweetheart." Okay, that fit-all name that had come so easily off his tongue definitely wouldn't help matters. "We can't do this."

"Of course we can." When she shimmied against him, despite orders to the contrary, his body immediately chose sides. *Her side.* "I may be a little tipsy—"

"I think the ship has sailed far past that," he reminded them both.

"Perhaps." She frowned. "Maybe a teensy bit." She lifted a hand, managing to hold her thumb and index finger a bit apart. "But I haven't had so much to drink that I've forgotten that there's one thing we're both very, very good at doing together."

"Still." There was no point in denying what was definitely true. "There are rules."

"I'm tired of rules." She leaned her head back and blinked, as if trying to focus her gaze on his. "I've spent most of my life trying to be a good girl. Which didn't stop my parents from being killed."

"That sucks."

As he knew all too well. At least he hadn't lost his father. Not that Colin Brannigan would have ever won a father-of-the-year award, but all of his sons had always known they'd had a home.

Having felt so alone his last years at the ranch, Finn had overlooked all those years that, while never exactly a home in the traditional family sense, it had been a place where all the Brannigan brothers had connected in a way they hadn't for a very long time.

"It does suck." She blew out a long, sad breath. Her eyes glistened. "Especially after the Wicked Witch of the West told those lies about me and had me arrested."

"You were arrested?" He'd learned long ago not to take anything anyone said while drunk literally. Which was another reason he wasn't much of a drinker. Whoever it was who'd said that "in wine was truth" had obviously hung out with a different crowd.

"Well, not technically arrested. Like with handcuffs and an ugly mug shot. But I was taken away from the Covingtons' house and stuck in foster care."

Okay. This was weird. Finn's dick gave up its argument and promptly deflated while his brain kicked into gear, trying to follow the slurred verbal breadcrumbs she was scattering about like those pink rose petals.

"The Covingtons? Are you talking about your fiancé's mother?"

"Former fiancé," she reminded him. "That's

the one." She nodded. Slowly but decidedly. "I lived with them."

"With the Covingtons?" Finn didn't remember any girl coming to the Christmas open houses with Dickhead IV, who was an only child.

"Uh huh." Her teeth worried her bottom lip as she started slanting toward starboard.

Taking hold of her shoulders, Finn straightened her back up. "Maybe you ought to sit down."

"I'm fine. And yes, the family took me in when my parents died. I think maybe Mr. Covington felt a little guilty." Her smooth brow furrowed as she seemed to be thinking back on what had to have been a horrific time. It also had him thinking that, as hard as losing his mom had been on him, the loss must've have been far worse for his older brothers. The ones who'd had more years to bond with her.

"I always thought she only went along with him because of how it would look," Tori said, breaking into Finn's sudden thought of how hard it must have been on James, especially, given that so much of taking care of his brothers had landed on his shoulders. "Tossing a poor eleven-year-old orphan out of the servants' cottage wouldn't have been seen as an act of charity."

"Servants?" Finn nearly looked up for the lightbulb clicking on over his head. "Your parents worked for the Covingtons?"

She nodded again. "Since before I was born."

"So that's how you met Carter IV."

"Yes." As if the topic wasn't her favorite—and why the hell would it be?—she stalled by kissing his chin. His cheek. Lips. "I loved him nearly all my life."

Seriously? Even that night *they'd* spent together? She hadn't been wearing a rock on her finger that night, but maybe she didn't wear an engagement ring while working because by looking single, and possibly available, she'd get more and bigger tips.

She hadn't seemed like the kind of woman to play guys like that. And Finn liked to think he was too smart and too experienced to be played. But then again, it hadn't taken any convincing to get her up to his suite.

"Of course, because he was older, he never noticed me." She slid out of his touch and wove her way over to the table where she'd left the glass. She picked up the bottle and refilled it again.

"I don't think that's a very good idea," he suggested.

"I thought you were a flyboy," she said, those full, sexy lips frowning at him over the rim of the flute. "Not shore patrol." She drank the champagne down and reached for the bottle again.

He beat her to it. Not that it took much effort, since her hand missed it on the first try. "I'm cutting you off."

She tossed up her chin. Her eyes cleared just long enough to flash sparks. "You're not a bartender. And you definitely don't own me."

She stated each word as if it had a period behind it.

"Point taken. But I do happen to be your friend."

She'd looked prepared to take off on him and try to grab the bottle again when those words sunk through the buzz. She blinked. One time. Two. A third. Slowly, like a serious owl. "Since when?"

"Damned if I know," he admitted. "Maybe since I arrived to find your Mt. Denali cake reduced to crumbs. Or earlier, when you climbed into my floatplane despite being afraid."

"I was not." She tossed her head. Then flinched. Oh, yeah. She was going to have one helluva headache in the morning.

"Weren't you?"

"No. I was merely concerned that your piloting skills might not live up to your Topgun ego."

"Ouch." He rubbed his chest. "Bull's-eye."

"Sorry. That was mean. Especially since I don't want to argue."

As her hands took hold of his belt again, he grabbed hold of them and held her arms out to her sides. Even as he was scrambling to figure out how to bail from this situation, he couldn't help noticing that she still had great arms. Which made sense. It probably took strength to carry that guitar around.

"You need to go to bed."

"I believe that's what I've been saying."

When the tip of her tongue came out to lick her lower lip, the blood started rushing from his brain down below that belt again. It was a good thing he hadn't planned to get married like all his brothers and have kids, because if his jeans heated up any more, they'd burst into flames, thus putting an end to any chance of him adding to the Brannigan genealogy.

"That's it." He scooped her up and threw her over his shoulder. "You are going to bed. Alone."

"That's no fun." She was upside down, her roving hands dangerously close to the back of his belt as she tugged up his shirt. "Besides, I tried sleeping. It didn't work. My mind just kept buzzing."

"You've had a long day. Plus, all this light can be a shock to the system when people first get up here," he said. "Your body gets out of sync and disrupts your circadian rhythms, especially if you've been traveling. And, although it's a little late for me to be telling you this, alcohol makes it worse."

"It's definitely too late for that," she surprised him by agreeing. "Unless this floor has taken to spinning."

"It's steady as a rock."

"I was afraid of that." She sighed as he put her down onto the bed. "I'm going to have a hangover in the morning, aren't I?"

"Probably."

How about the mother of all hangovers? At her weight, the amount of alcohol she'd ingested would have been multiplied. Concerned, Finn had decided to spend the night on the couch, to keep track of her, when her skin turned an unhealthy shade of green.

"Oh, no!"

He'd been there, done that enough times to know what was about to happen. Scooping her up again, he carried her into the bathroom, just in time.

10

FEELING BOTH SICK as a dog and horribly embarrassed, Tori knelt over the commode and barfed up the worst-looking blue and purple mess she'd ever seen. That's what she got for eating a mountain then tossing champagne on top of it. She was wondering why the hell she hadn't just decided to take up flame eating while she was at it when she realized that Finn was not only still in the bathroom but—oh, God—he was crouched on the tile floor beside her, holding her hair back with one hand while rubbing the nape of her neck with the other.

Could her life get any worse? Adding to the adulterous, scheming fiancé, no home and no money to pay for one thanks to the cratering of her bank account, running into the one man she'd never been able to forget, only to hurl up her guts after sexually attacking him. And, adding insult to injury, being turned down.

Did he have to be so nice?

She flushed the toilet and started to get up again, his hand moving from the back of her neck to her elbow to steady her, when the second wave came.

Her moan was like a wounded animal as she waved him away, dropped back down, and humiliated herself even more until there was nothing left but dry heaves.

Wishing she could just flush herself away, or hey, maybe an earthquake would suddenly open up and swallow her—hadn't she read about some major faults up here?—she collapsed into a puddle on the floor.

"Wait here," he said.

No problem. Tori wasn't certain she'd ever be able to move again.

She closed her eyes, which only encouraged more spinning, and opened them to see him at the sink, wetting a small hand towel. Then he was back, helping her into a sitting position, her back against the wall, as he gently washed her face with the cool, wet cloth.

"I think I'm going to die," she moaned.

"No." He stroked the cloth over her forehead. Her cheeks. Beneath her eyes, which were still having a problem focusing. "Though you may wish you had in the morning."

"You'll probably never believe this, but I've never gotten drunk enough to throw up before."

"You've probably never had a marriage breakup before it started, either."

"No. That was a first."

He dampened her lips, which felt as dry as the Sahara. "Like going up to a certain flyboy's suite was a first?"

"I was just going to thank you for being a gentleman. Until you brought that up," she muttered.

"Sorry." He rubbed her shoulders, soothing the muscles that had gone from lax to stiff as boards at the reminder of that other night she'd allowed herself a freedom she'd learned to keep tightly reined in. "But it's good you got a lot of that out of your system. Ready to go back to bed?"

She nodded, then wished she hadn't when a lightning bolt hit behind her eye. "Alone," she accepted his earlier dictate. Not that it would probably matter. After this gross incidence, she doubted he'd ever want to have sex with her again.

Which was what she wanted.

And wasn't this a fine mess she'd gotten herself into? Now she was not only a wretchedly ugly drunk. She was also a liar.

✦   ✦   ✦

SINCE ARRIVING IN Caribou, Finn had gotten

used to the constant sunshine, but after that episode with Tori, he was too wired to go home. Even if he could sleep, with his luck, he'd have nightmares of being back in the skies trying to dodge that SAM or skidding off the carrier. Or dreaming of having sex with Tori. Which wouldn't count as a nightmare since it had been great, but as much as he still wanted her, he didn't want it to be a rebound situation.

So, where did that leave him?

Not having an answer to that, he drove to the Caribou Café, which had started out a hundred years ago as a small diner that served the most basic meals to miners and dog sled mushers. It had grown since then, especially after Barbara Ann had bought the rest of the connected buildings on the block, adding a tavern/pool hall, a music venue with a dance floor, and the Trading Post, which served as a grocery store and post office.

Never one to rest on her laurels, she'd then bought a vacant working man's hotel across the street and fixed it up into a bed-and-breakfast that offered dinner delivery from the café. In one way she reminded Finn of his father. The woman simply didn't stop, running at full tilt all the time.

Yet she always took time to ask people how they were doing and actually cared about the answer. He'd heard it said that the reason she'd found her true home in Alaska was because there wasn't anywhere else in the country big enough to hold her large, generous heart. Which, of course, explained the explosion of pink that had resulted in Tori's meltdown.

The café wasn't that fancy. The rustic wooden tables were two, four, and six tops, the few booths were covered in scratched brown leather, and the floor was a vintage rough-scraped yellow cedar locally milled of the kind builders down in the lower forty-nine were paying big bucks to reclaim from barns, mills, and other old buildings. In a bit of what Finn took to be theme restaurant chic, old mining equipment hung down from the rafters, and painted totems brightened the log walls.

One of the place's design functions was that, while the café and Gold Gulch Saloon flowed into each other in one long, open space, each had its own exterior entry to the sidewalk. Finn chose the one to the tavern, wove through the tables and past the two pool tables, and slid onto a stool next to Yazz at the long, scarred wooden bar.

"Why aren't you home with Hannah?" he asked the pilot who'd gotten married last New Year's and was still in that starry-eyed honeymoon stage.

"She's out of town." Yazz, a native Alaskan who wore his hair in two long black braids, tipped back his beer. "At a medical convention in Seattle. She's determined to bring back a partner. Preferably a board certified ob-gyn."

Being that Hannah Yazzie was Caribou's sole family practitioner, Finn knew from talking with the pilot that her job was often twenty-four seven. Finn figured she could've made big bucks staying in Seattle after graduating from University of Washington Medical School. Yet she'd chosen UW because it was tops in the nation in primary and rural care, which was where her heart lay. A heart that had led her here to Caribou, and Yazz.

"My money's on her." He glanced over at a group of sport fisherman at a nearby table lying about today's catch. From the spread of one guy's arms, he must've landed Moby Dick. "Business is good," he said to the bartender who'd returned to behind the taps after delivering a tray of tequila shots to another group across the room.

"Booming," the bartender, Cody Waggoner, whom Finn had discovered had a PhD in physics from MIT, agreed. "Which gives true meaning to making hay while the sun shines. The usual?"

Finn glanced over at Yazz's golden Alaskan Summer Ale, considered it, and decided he'd had enough changes in routine for one day. "Yeah. Thanks."

"You've got it." He popped the top, then put a bottle of amber in front of Finn, along with a bowl of bar nuts. "I heard you brought in a runaway bride today."

"Word gets around." Finn took a long swallow, then scooped up a handful of nuts.

"Small towns," Yazz said. "Barbara Ann's feathers are definitely ruffled. She wanted to go out there and personally apologize, but Mary talked her out of it."

"Yeah. That wouldn't have been the best idea," Finn agreed.

Tori's appearance in town had already landed her on the gossip line. The last thing she needed was to have anyone show up as she was in the process of killing the mountain cake. Or worse yet, barfing it up.

"So, how's she doing?" Cody asked.

"When I left, she'd gone to bed."

"Must be a bummer to be alone on what was supposed to be her wedding night," Yazz said, a gleam of satisfied memory in his dark eyes that neared the point of TMI as far as Finn was concerned.

Finn merely shrugged and took another drag on the beer.

"I heard she's famous," another patron, seated on the other side of Yazz, broke into the conversation. "Barbara Ann's put her on the juke."

"Seriously?"

The typical genre played in the Gold Gulch

was country. The old kind, like Cash and Waylon, with a few of the more pop stuff tossed into the mix for the women who liked to dance to it. Which, Finn heard, helped up the bar tabs since there probably wasn't a guy on the planet who'd object to women shaking their badonkadonks.

"Yep." Yazz's eyes narrowed, daring Finn to offer a word of objection. "Hannah likes her songs."

"She's got a great voice." Finn's body started heating up at the memory of that silky soprano singing in his ear.

"You listen to folk music?" Cody asked.

"Something wrong with that?" Finn countered.

"Not at all." It must have come out harsher than he'd intended because the bartender raised his hands. "I just figured you more for a head banger rocker."

"You've been watching too many war flicks," Finn said. "In reality pilots have too much to do while we're in the cockpit to rock out to Van Halen."

"Well, fuck. Guess that screws up me having any Navy career," the guy sitting next to Yazz said. "Since that and using the uniform to get all the chicks I want would be the only reasons to join up."

Finn didn't bother to point out that with a probable body mass index equal to a walrus, the guy couldn't fit in a cockpit.

"How long is she staying?" Cody asked as he washed some glasses in the sink behind the bar.

"Beats me. She didn't share her plans." Which wasn't the truth, the whole truth, and nothing but the truth, but if tonight's behavior was any indication, she probably wasn't settling into Caribou.

"Her fiancé booked the cabin for two weeks."

"Then I guess that's how long she'll stay."

"Should give you time to close the deal," a guy two stools down from Finn piped up.

"That's not in my plans."

"She came here thinking about having two weeks of nonstop honeymoon monkey sex," walrus guy said with a leer. "You've already got the inside track, having met her first, but if you don't do her, there are lots of guys in town who'd be glad to take on the assignment."

Feeling his teeth grind to dust, Finn took another long drink to cool his temper, which was beginning to heat up. "She's a nice woman."

"Didn't say she wasn't. But whatever the hell happened to have her up here alone, she's likely in the market for some revenge sex."

"How about we drop the damn topic and watch some hockey?" Cody said, putting an end to the conversation by turning the TV to a rerun of this year's Stanley Cup final.

"Just sayin'," the guy muttered.

"Anyone ever tell you that you're a real piece of work?" Finn asked.

"My wife. All the time. Why do you think I spend so much damn time here, increasing Barbara Ann's bank account?"

Finn polished off his beer, watched a replay of the Pittsburg Penguins beat the San Jose Sharks (who, to his mind, should've been called Land Sharks, and why would you play hockey in California, anyway?), and reminded himself that despite not having been able to get her out of his mind, Tori Cassidy was trouble. He'd be wise to keep his distance.

Which would, if she went ahead and stayed in Caribou for the entire two weeks, be easier said than done.

Meaning, he thought glumly, that he'd landed himself in a whole wide world of hurt.

11

THE KNOCK AT the door sounded like a jackhammer. Rolling over onto her stomach with a moan, Tori covered her head with the pillow.

It continued.

She ignored it. Just as she tried to ignore her head, where a crew of lumberjacks had taken up residence and were attacking her with chainsaws.

When she finally realized whoever it was was going to keep adding to the cacophony, she stumbled out of bed, and, trying to blink a desert's worth of sand out of her gritty eyes, she dragged her sorry butt to the door.

And was immediately blinded by the bright rays of a sun that hit like a fireball. But not so blinded she couldn't see Finn standing on the front porch.

"I was running along the lakefront and thought I'd drop by to make sure you're still alive," he said.

"Depends on what your definition of alive is," she countered. When his glance moved to her hair, she realized she undoubtedly had the worst bedhead ever. Her hair on a good morning made her look like a wild woman. This morning was a very long way from a good one.

"Given how hammered you were last night, I figured you could use some hangover juju."

"I wasn't that hammered."

At least she hoped she hadn't been as she glanced around the room. The balloons had drifted down from the rafters and were lying, half-deflated, on the floor, looking about as bad as she felt. Gilt confetti was everywhere, even in her hair as she ran her fingers through it, and cake crumbs were scattered with it all over the floor. And speaking of the cake... It looked as if it had been attacked by a pack of wolves. Or Bigfoot.

"You were three sheets to the wind when you coerced me into dancing with you," he corrected easily as he slipped by her into the house.

Dancing? "I don't remember inviting you in."

"Ah, but I come bearing gifts." He held up a paper bag. "The world's best hangover cure."

"I don't have a hangover."

"Yeah, you do. But don't worry, in no time, you'll feel great." As if he had every right to make himself right at home, Finn walked into the kitchen, pulled a glass from the open shelves, and poured some purple-blue liquid from a plastic bottle in his bag into it.

"A magic elixir," he said, digging another, smaller white bottle out of the bag. Then a brown one. "Unlike some of those hangover recipes that make you gag—"

"Please." She held up a hand as her stomach turned. "I'd appreciate you not using that word."

He tilted his head, gave her face, which she knew had gone pale as she'd felt the blood leave it, a judicious look. "Point taken. Anyway, you need to hydrate, and this not only tastes like a glacial waterfall, it'll replace those electrolytes you lost even better than water can."

He shook two pills out of the white bottle and another from the brown. "Ibuprofen for the buzz saw in your head and a B-vitamin complex to replace minerals and vitamins. Sit down, take those, and I'll make some coffee."

"Are you always this bossy?" She stayed standing.

"Actually, you're talking about my brother, Perfect James the Elder," he said. "I'm probably one of the most easygoing of the seven of us. Except for maybe Knox, who everyone thought was just a surfer dude-slash-bartender but surprised the hell of us when he turned out to be this entrepreneur." He shrugged. "Shows you never know."

He took hold of her hand, turned it over, and dropped the pills into her palm. "This will be a good start. Then you can take a long, hot shower to sweat some more of the alcohol out, and I'll take you into town for a big breakfast of steak and eggs."

"I don't eat breakfast." Just the thought of any food, let alone such heavy ones, caused her stomach to start doing flips.

"All you've had since lunch yesterday is cake. Which, no offense to Kendra Graham, who owns Mountain Munchies and created a really cool dessert, but you probably managed to down close to a five-pound bag of sugar. Especially when you factor in the additional sugar in nearly a bottle of champagne. So, you need some protein, fat, and carbs in your stomach. And getting out in the fresh air will clear your head, raise your endorphins, and generally make you feel better."

Getting out in the fresh air and all that sunshine could probably kill her. What she needed was to get back to bed. Fortunately, she hadn't killed off all her brain cells, because she managed to avoid sharing that thought.

"You sound as if you have some experience," she said instead.

"Hello." He waved his hand in front of her still gritty, blurry eyes. "I was in the Navy, remember? We can drink all the other services under the table."

She might be out, but she wasn't dead yet. She lifted her chin and shot him her most skeptical look. "I'll bet not SEALs."

"Especially SEALs," he said. "Max, he's another one of my brothers, just happens to have been a SEAL. Those guys don't have any body fat to absorb the alcohol. They may be lean, mean assassins of terrorists. But believe me, they're the first to go down like a Sitka Spruce in a typhoon after a few tequila shots."

Tori wasn't sure she believed him about that. She had, after all, seen *Zero Dark Thirty* and read a bunch of romance novels featuring SEAL heroes. Which, admittedly, were fiction, but still she could tell the authors had done their research. Still, she wasn't so hungover that she couldn't hear the affection in Finn's tone as he spoke of his brothers. Including the so-called bossy, perfect one.

Once again, she envied him having experienced what sounded like a rich, wonderful family life.

"I think I'll take that shower," she said. "Thanks for bringing by the care package. But I'll be fine."

"You're already fine," he said, a gleam of what appeared to be honest masculine appreciation in his eyes. "I'll make the coffee while you get ready to go out."

"You're a liar," she said without heat. "Because I have to look like death warmed over. And I'm not going anywhere."

"Then we're at a stalemate," he said with a slow, too-sexy smile. "Because neither am I."

"I'm not having sex with you." Where did that come from? Oh, yeah, despite it perhaps being the last thing she did before dying, she wanted to do exactly that.

"Well, damn." He put his hand over his heart, which drew her attention to his hard, ripped chest. Not that she hadn't already noticed. Or forgotten. "There goes my plan for the morning. I guess I'll just have to settle for breakfast."

"You're not the boss of me. And we're not having breakfast," she repeated. To his back, because he'd already gone back into the kitchen.

Deciding to deal with Finn Brannigan later, Tori tossed her head, wishing she hadn't, and left the room.

A THOUGHT OCCURRED to Tori while she was standing beneath the dual sprays, reveling in the hot water pounding against her body like a Swedish masseuse she'd once gone to after pulling a shoulder muscle taking her Taylor down from an overhead bus rack.

How could she not remember eating all that cake? Or drinking a bottle of champagne? Especially how could she not remember dancing with Finn? Which brought up another thought.

Jumping out of the shower, she grabbed a towel, took a few quick swipes over her body, and since her skin seemed super oversensitized, changed into her most comfortable underwear, a pair of leggings, and a blue Music in the Mountains T-shirt from a folk music festival she'd played in southern Oregon.

Cringing at the roar that reverberated like a jet engine in her head, she blew her hair dry just enough to pull it into a ponytail. Then, taking a deep breath to steady herself, she went back into the front room, where Finn was standing at the window, a white mug with the Mt. Denali National Park logo in his hand, looking out at the mountain that defined the town.

"I need to know something," she said.

He turned and swept an appreciative look over her. It was strange how some guys checking her out could make her feel creepy. But not when he did it. Maybe, she admitted, because from that first moment their eyes had met, literally across a crowded ballroom, she'd wanted him to look at her. But definitely not the way she must have looked last night.

"About last night."

"Okay." He arched one brow—how did people do that?—and kept his gaze on hers as he took a drink of coffee.

"You said we danced."

"We did."

"Slow or fast?"

"Definitely slow."

Not good.

"In a fashion," he tacked on. "You were a little unsteady on your feet by the time I showed up."

Oh, no. An unwilling memory flashed through her mind of her arms twined around his neck, of pressing herself against his body, begging him, no, *demanding* that he have sex with her.

It could be a false memory. A fantasy. Or a leftover fragment from an alcohol-sodden dream.

"We didn't do..." Wouldn't she have remembered that? "I mean, it was just dancing, right?"

"Well"—he shrugged with a quirk of his lips—"there might have been a kiss." He wickedly paused a beat. "With a bit of tongue involved." Then, as if taking pity on her misery, he shook his head. "That's all. Nothing more happened."

Which was a relief. Unless, of course, you counted her hurling up all that cake and champagne. She could have thrown up all over him while dancing. Or kissing.

The conversation triggered a foggy memory of him being the one who'd stopped things from getting out of hand.

"Thank you."

Even though she wanted to go back to bed, pull the covers over her head, and hide out here forever, or at least until the cabin reservation ran out, Tori reminded herself that she'd managed to overcome much more than mere embarrassment. She'd been born with a knack for songwriting. And singing. But her strongest talent, which she'd honed to the strength of tempered steel over the years, was the ability to keep moving on. This certainly wasn't the worst thing to happen to her in the last year. Month. Even this week.

"No problem." He gave her a long look. "Ready to go?"

She was about to tell him that she'd go where she wanted, when she wanted, and right now, she didn't want any damn breakfast. But, on the other hand—and wasn't there always another hand?—Tori had known her share of losers over the years. It was like she had power that attracted them. Which was why she'd thought having a rational agreement with Carter had been the solution.

And how wrong had she been about that? The thing was, Finn had acted like a true officer and a gentleman. Which meant that she sort of owed him this win.

"I'm not eating steak," she said as she picked up her purse from the table by the inner front door.

His only response was a shrug of those wide, military male shoulders. But the grin he flashed her didn't bother to hide the fact that he'd never expected the argument to go any other way.

12

THEY'D NO SOONER walked through the inner door of the Caribou Café than an older, rounded blond woman, who could have been Paula Deen's separated-at-birth twin, came rushing out from behind the counter.

"I'm so sorry," she said, wrapping Tori in a big hug. "I was only trying to give you a special night. As soon as Mary Muldoon—she owns Osprey Air—told me about the reservation change, I was going to rush right over there, but unfortunately, she told me that Finn had already landed at the lake…

"I tried to call him, but he had his phone off. *Again.*" She shot him a laser-sharp look that appeared to bounce right off him.

"Even if some calls could go through when I'm in the air, I wouldn't take them," he said. "It's too much of a distraction."

She placed a hand on her hip. "Did I mention Mary told me you had *landed?* So you weren't in the air at the time."

She might be wearing a hot pink tunic over a pair of cropped flowered pants, and her voice might be drenched in the round, soft vowels of the Carolina Lowcountry, but Tori had spent enough time in the South to recognize a genuine steel magnolia when she saw one.

"I must have forgotten to turn it back on," he responded in a bland tone that didn't fool anyone.

"You never turn it on because you don't want to talk to anyone," Barbara Ann Carter said.

"There is that," Finn agreed.

"Well." She huffed out a frustrated breath. Then turned her attention back to Tori. "I'm Barbara Ann Carter, who left you that misguided welcome note.'"

"Don't worry about it. It's nice to meet you," Tori said, knowing that Finn was right about the woman's heart being in the right place. "As I guess you already figured out, I'm Tori Cassidy."

"Bless your heart, I certainly do know that." She shot Finn another look. "Isn't she sweet as pie?"

"Or cake." A wicked spark in his eyes as he looked toward Tori suggested he was thinking of that sugary kiss they'd shared.

"Oh, let's not bring that up." Barbara Ann waved off his reference. "Poor Kendra worked so hard on that cake."

"It was beautiful," Tori assured her. "And tasty."

"She's a dynamite baker." Her brow furrowed. "Unfortunately, she told me she can't cook worth beans."

Before Tori could figure out why that was relevant to the conversation, the café owner switched gears. "I was so excited when Mary told me you were coming to Caribou," she gushed. "I have most of your songs on the jukebox in the Gold Gulch next door."

Tori's gaze followed the tilt of the teased blond head toward the far wall, which opened to a log room like this one. But along with the colorful totems, like the ones standing up against the log walls of the café, there were also a number of wild animal heads. Which had Tori wondering exactly how the restaurant owner sourced her menu.

"I wouldn't think mine would be the type your customers would go for," she said.

Which was an understatement. Having been inspired by singer-songwriters like Joni Mitchell and Carole King, and more recently, Jaspar Lepak, with whom she'd sung a duet at the Music in the Mountains festival, Tori's songs were about love, life, and relationships. Both the good and the bad, and what even the most intelligent women would occasionally be willing to sacrifice for love. Not, she considered, the type of message a guy would want to ponder while drinking a draft beneath the unblinking marble eye of a dead moose.

"You'd be right as rain about that," Barbara Ann allowed as she led them to a table by the window that offered yet another stunning view of the mountains. "Most of our good ole boys go for old time crying-in-your-beer country. Some of the younger ones go for metal, but they usually end up at the Loaded Loon.

"But women like songs about love and life, especially the getting-even ones, which you can probably relate to firsthand. So, by putting them on the juke, I get the gals, who are outnumbered by guys in this state, coming in. The gals, in turn, bring in more guys. Which is good for business and everyone's happy."

"That's smart."

"Thank you." The woman patted her hair. "Although things are better than when I showed up here as a naïve eighteen-year-old bride, we females haven't reached full equality yet. Which is why, I suppose, the good Lord gave us more brains."

She pulled two laminated menus from behind the sugar jar. "You look a little peaked after your long trip yesterday," she said sympathetically. "I'll get you some coffee while you peruse the menu and decide. When you're ready, holler. Of course, if there's anything special you'd like, just ask, and I'll fix it special for you."

"I'm sure that won't be necessary," Tori said, glancing down at the bright photos of the various meals. The breakfast offerings seemed fairly standard, with one surprise for this part of the world. "You have grits."

"With cheese or without," the café owner said. "For lunch and dinner, I add in some shrimp. Of course, truth be told, they're basically a butter and salt delivery system, but a dish of cheesy grits can perk you up faster than greased lightning."

Only five minutes ago, Tori would've sworn she wouldn't be able to eat a thing. But the familiar food had her taste buds perking up. She'd first discovered the dish at a low-cost waffle chain that was a favorite of musicians across the Southern states looking for a late-night breakfast after a gig.

"I'll have the grits without cheese, please." No point in pushing things. "And two scrambled eggs with whole wheat toast, no butter."

"You might as well have the butter since you're getting a tub in the grits," Barbara Ann advised. She swept a look over Tori. "And it's not like you have to worry about a few pounds, given that you're a banana."

"A banana?"

"The way I see it, women fall into three types.

Bananas, apples, and pears. I was a banana myself until menopause settled in. Now I'm an apple." She ran her hands down over her curves. "JLo is a pear. While you're definitely a banana."

Tori cast a quick glance at Finn, who seemed to be biting the inside of his cheek to keep from laughing. "I've never thought of it that way before," she said.

"Most bananas never do," Barbara Ann said. "I didn't when I was your age, although you've got the looks of a girl who'll end up a banana for life. Would you like some cream in your coffee?" She switched topics without a blink of her mascaraed lashes.

Although Tori tended to drink her coffee black because it was easier to add to a group order on the road, she decided that after eating a mountain of cake, even if she had lost most of it, she deserved to indulge herself. "Thanks, I would."

Without looking at the menu, Finn ordered the steak and eggs, hash browns, a short stack of pancakes, and link sausage.

"Sounds as if you eat here often," Tori said as Barbara Ann bustled off to get their orders.

"If you don't count takeout deli from the Trading Post, or desserts, this is the only place in town," he said. "I don't really cook so, since I'd rather not live on cold cereal, the Caribou's easier."

"Makes sense." Glancing over at an order being delivered to a nearby booth, she decided she'd hate to see his arteries.

He followed her gaze. "It's basic. But Barbara Ann has built herself a small empire knowing what folks want and giving it to them. Like the music. And what beer and liquor she serves. She does order in more craft beer during the summer, since tourists are willing to pay more on vacation, but after Labor Day, you're going to see a lot more Buds than the artisan stuff."

"I doubt I'll be here after Labor Day." Not wanting to think about being homeless in less than two weeks, she smiled up at Barbara Ann, who'd delivered their coffee in two thick white mugs with a moose on the front. "Thank you," she said.

"You're very welcome. I got the beans special for the summer crowd," she said, confirming what Finn had said about her buying habits. "They're fair trade from Costa Rica, and although they cost a bit more, they're proving so popular with the locals I'll probably continue them through the year.

"I'm seriously considering buying the empty storefront across the street next to my B and B, getting one of those fancy Italian espresso machines, hiring a barista, and going into business with Kendra, who could supply some muffins and doughnuts. We could become Seattle North."

Her lips, wearing a bright pink that matched as her tunic, curved in a big smile. "Y'all enjoy now, and I'll be getting your meal out in two shakes."

"I like her," Tori said, watching as the woman stopped by each table on her way back to the kitchen.

"Everyone does. Like I said, not only does she own most of the town, I get the feeling that no one who's been here a while could imagine Caribou without her."

"That's nice." After pouring in some cream from the white pitcher that matched the mugs, she took a sip of the coffee and found it every bit as good as promised. "To have a place where you fit in."

"Yeah. I guess."

Tori thought that was an odd response coming from a man with such a large family, but not wanting to comment, which would only bring her own past into the conversation, she merely took a longer drink of the lightened coffee.

Between the drink Finn had forced down her, the coffee, and the pills, Tori was starting to feel more like a human being. But not so much that she felt inclined to carry on a casual conversation. Especially with a man she'd been naked with.

Which was why, after Barbara Ann delivered two large platters, along with Finn's side dishes, she was grateful that he seemed willing to eat in silence. Outside, just as they finished, gray clouds moved across the blue sky, bringing rain that streamed down the windows.

"I should probably go shopping for a slicker," she said. The butter and sugar had conspired to give her a boost she knew would probably wear off in a way that had her crashing, but for now, she was going to enjoy the rush of renewed energy. "I know Alaska's far north, but I expected more summer weather."

"It's a lot more changeable than L.A.," he said. "We can stop by the Trading Post on the way back to your cabin."

"That's not necessary."

"You'll need rain gear." He reached into his wallet, pulled out some bills he put on the table. Then stood up and amazed her by pulling out her chair. Tori couldn't remember the last time anyone other than a maître d' had done that for her, and that had only been the few times Carter had risked taking her out to a restaurant where they might run into his family or someone he knew. "And the Trading Post is on the way."

He was doing it again. Doing his alpha-male-in-charge thing, but she wasn't going to risk calling attention to them by arguing. After waving good-bye to Barbara Ann, who was ringing up a family of five, Finn and Tori left the restaurant.

She'd just buckled her seat belt when she belatedly saw the sign in the window.

"Wait a minute." Unfastening the belt, she jumped back down to the sidewalk and, having hopefully found the answer to her problems, ran back into the café.

13

WONDERING WHAT THE hell had lit her fire, Finn followed Tori into the café.

"They're in the kitchen," the morning shift waitress, who, Finn had heard through the Osprey grapevine, was coming off a divorce to a mountain guide, said. She tilted her head toward the swinging door.

John Black, a Grizzly Adams lookalike who'd once been the cook for a fishing boat out of Dutch Harbor, was frying up some sausage with one hand while flipping eggs with the other. Over in the corner by the prep table, he saw the two women. Whatever point Tori was so enthusiastically making, Barbara Ann appeared openly skeptical.

"Look," Tori was saying as he approached, "have you seen the movie *Julie and Julia*?"

"The one where the girl blogger makes every dish in Julia Child's *Mastering the Art of French Cooking* in one year?"

"That's it!" Finn hadn't seen Tori Cassidy that excited about anything since that night on Coronado when he'd located her G-spot on the first try and sent her flying. "I'm the Amy Adams character. I've made every one of those five hundred and twenty-four dishes. Though not in a single year," she admitted.

"Well, now, darlin', that's real impressive," Barbara Ann said. "But that still doesn't mean that you could cook what people hereabouts want to eat."

"They eat meat, don't they?"

Like, duh, Finn thought. Mary had warned him that if he thought summer tourism season was busy, he hadn't been through the fall game hunting season.

"Well, of course they do."

"*Boeuf bourguignon* wasn't always haute cuisine," Tori argued. "It was a basic peasant dish that works wonderfully with venison and I'll bet would work with just about any game meat. And that's just for starters."

"That's real interesting, but—"

"I can make a bourbon-glazed duck breast that's a lot more interesting than chicken or turkey. And if you buy from local hunters, you could charge more and maintain a higher profit margin.

"And you have grouse up here, right?"

"Lots of different ones," the other woman allowed.

"How does grouse stuffed with apples, sausage, and chanterelles sound?"

"Fancy."

"It does. But it's one of many ways French hunters would cook it. Julia taught that French food is good, basic country food people ate. It's just the snooty restauranteurs who figured out that they could make more money if they intimidated diners into thinking that it was too complex for the average home cook."

"I make a mean bowl of grits," Barbara Ann argued. "Which is pretty much what fancy places pass off as polenta. And I can make sausage."

"See, you're halfway there. You can get fresh apples, right?"

"Of course."

"And mushrooms?"

"With all our rain and cloudy skies, we've got tons of those. I buy 'em local for mushroom omelets."

"You're already set."

"It sounds tasty." Finn could hear the borough's most successful entrepreneur softening.

"It is."

"But you want to tell me how you're going to get folks around here to even try French food?"

"Easy." Tori folded her arms beneath her

breasts. "We don't tell them it's French."

Barbara Ann chewed on the tip of a pink fingernail. Finn could see the wheels turning inside that opportunistic blond head. "If they don't ask, we don't tell."

"Exactly!" Tori exhaled a huge breath that hinted she was claiming victory. A bit too soon.

"I still don't have any way of knowing that you really can pull that off," Barbara Ann said. "Not that I'm accusing you of being untruthful, understand, but it's been difficult enough running this kitchen ever since Patti decided to up and marry that park ranger who got transferred down to the Grand Canyon.

"They're leaving in a week and I've got too much to do to be cooking every night without a backup cook for John. And while we'll never do the business that Anchorage or even Juneau does, I don't want to have to deal with a learning curve in the middle of tourist season."

"That makes perfect sense," Tori agreed, getting back into the fight. Considering that she still had to be dealing with a hangover, Finn admired her tenacity. "So, how about you give me a trial run? Without pay."

Since, despite her warm and caring heart, the older woman was known to squeeze her pennies, that got her attention. Sticking with the earlier hunting theme, she reminded Finn of a German pointer who'd just scented a ruffled grouse.

"You're a singer. A good one. Why would you be willing to spend your nights in this hot kitchen?"

"How much would you pay me to sing in the Gold Gulch?" Tori countered.

"Not as much as I'd pay you to cook in the café," Barbara allowed. "It's not that you're not worth it, but—"

"Having sung solely for tips before, I get it," Tori said. "Performing has never been the most stable way to make a living. Which is why I didn't suggest it. But I'm in a bit of a financial bind right now, so let me throw in a sweetener."

Damn if this hadn't turned into a serious business negotiation. Finn knew that the sight of Tori's teeth biting her full, rosy bottom lip shouldn't turn him on. But it did.

"One week free cooking as a trial," Tori suggested. "I can send you a list of menu suggestions and ingredients you'd need beforehand. Then, when you hire me, which you will, four nights cooking, and a one-hour concert on my night off for tips."

Wide blue eyes narrowed. "That financial bind you mentioned. Is that fiancé who didn't show up with you the one who put you in it?"

"Not solely. But yes, he's part of my situation. The other reason is that my recording company went bankrupt and my contract has been put up for sale by the receivers. Since I can't afford to buy them back, I'm essentially starting over."

"Okay." Barbara put both hands on her hips, stared up at the ceiling for a long moment, then said, "Here's my offer. You go back to the cabin and email me your two best dishes along with ingredients. Nothing I can't easily source out of Anchorage. I'll cost it out, and since you're doing dinner, you can go a bit higher, but no more than thirty percent. And don't worry, if what you're suggesting doesn't make me a profit, I'll be sure to tell you beforehand." She rattled off an AlaskaMail address.

"I can do that," Tori said. "I'll make sure it's seasonal, to help keep the cost down."

"I've had professional cooks who've come here who didn't think about that while costing out a menu," Barbara Ann said. "You sure you've never cooked commercially before?"

"I partly put myself through community college making pub grub at a place in West Hollywood."

"So, you're talking wings, fries, and sliders. Which is a long way from what you're suggesting I add to the café's menu."

"I didn't plan the pub's menu," Tori allowed. "But I did talk the owner into adding fish tacos. It was L.A.," she pointed out with a return of what

Finn took as a bit of the humor he'd enjoyed that night they'd spent together. "As for seasonal costing, I learned about that from being addicted to the Food Network."

Barbara barked a laugh, then glanced over at Finn. "I like this one," she said. Then she was back to business. "Two nights' trial, starting Tuesday of next week. We're closed on Monday. If you're even half as good as you say, you'll cook four nights a week during the summer and hunting season if you're still around by fall.

"Three nights if you go into winter. And two thirty-minute shows on one of your off nights."

She named a figure that sounded low to Finn, who'd watched Tori perform before a full house of six hundred Navy brass and spouses in that hotel ballroom, but apparently it was more than Tori had expected because she'd blinked. Then flashed a smile bright enough to keep Caribou lit up all winter.

"You've got yourself a singing cook."

14

"I 'M IMPRESSED," HE said once they were back in the Jeep. "Both by the cooking stuff and your ability to negotiate with Barbara Ann."

Tori shrugged. "I need a job. She needs a cook. It was pretty much a no-brainer."

"Still, she's no pushover. Did you really make all those dishes?"

"I don't lie."

"I wasn't saying that." He lifted his hands after pressing the ignition button. "Okay, I guess I did. But I didn't mean it like it sounded."

"It was a reasonable enough question. It sounds impossible, which was why I was surprised when they made that true story movie. I thought I was the only person crazy enough to try to do that."

"Well, you're definitely going to be bringing in more business when the word gets out. Did you cook while you lived with the Covingtons?"

Tori's blood went cold. "How did you know

about that?"

"You told me last night. Not about the cooking." He pulled into the traffic, which was busier than she would have expected. But given that half the vehicles appeared to be seniors in RVs, she decided both Barbara Ann and Finn hadn't exaggerated about the influx of business during the summer season. "You said something about being arrested but not arrested."

"It's a long story. And no, I didn't cook while I was there. But my mother did. She was the Covingtons' housekeeper."

"Yeah. I figured that part out. I also got that you'd loved the son all your life."

"It was only a girlish crush." How much had she told him? "And before you point out that I'm no longer a girl, I realize that. It was just..." She rubbed the back of her neck. "Complicated," she said finally.

"So I gathered." He pulled into a parking space that had opened up in front of a wooden building. "Let's get your slicker. Then I'll take you back to the cabin and go to work. I've got a full list of passengers waiting for a bird's-eye view of the Alaskan interior."

As they left the Jeep, Tori wished she could believe his casual tone. Surely Finn had to wonder. Not just about what she'd drunkenly claimed to be an arrest—which had certainly felt like it at the time—but whether she'd been involved with Carter when she'd spent the night with him. Although she'd rather throw herself off Mt. Denali than talk about all that, neither did she want him to think she'd been sleeping around on Carter. Who, excuse me, certainly hadn't had any qualms about doing exactly that to her.

Since she appeared to be staying in Caribou at least long enough to replenish her bank account, she was probably going to have to explain.

But fortunately, thanks to all those tourists waiting for sightseeing flights, not today.

✧   ✧   ✧

IF FINN WAS going to list his top ten favorite things to do, not only would shopping not appear on the list, it wouldn't show up on the top hundred. So he was relieved when Tori snagged herself an inexpensive, lightweight, hooded red slicker within five minutes of entering the Trading Post. They did waste another couple minutes arguing over him having the jacket put on his account, but he'd managed to convince her that it was merely a loan until she got her first paycheck. The fact that she'd backed down so fast told him that she wasn't exaggerating when she'd told Barbara Ann she was in a financial bind.

She didn't say anything on the drive back to the lake. Which, he figured, meant that she was thinking about recipes for the café. Or more likely, how to avoid any discussion of Covington, her engagement, or anything having to do with their night together. Which, if he had any sense, he'd want to stay away from, too. The problem with that was, from the time he'd walked into that ballroom, it seemed as if he hadn't had a choice where Tori Cassidy was concerned.

When he pulled up in front of the cabin, she unfastened her seat belt and was about to make a run for it.

Let her go, his brain shouted.

Not yet, other parts of his body argued.

She's fragile, his conscience chimed in to back up his brain. Which was exactly what Mary had warned.

"Not yet." Even knowing he was getting in over his head, Finn caught her by the sleeve of that new cardinal-red slicker.

She turned back and glanced down at his hand on her arm. Then looked up. Finn could feel the sizzle as their gazes met, and from the slight tremble he felt beneath his fingers, he knew that she felt it, too.

"I thought you had passengers waiting."

"I do." He reached across the console and tucked an errant curl that had escaped that ponytail behind her ear. "Five senior citizens looking to check an air tour of the largest mountain in North America off their bucket list."

"You'd better go then." The back of her neck warmed beneath his stroking touch. "You never know how much time they have left. It's called a bucket list for a reason."

"It takes all of ten minutes to get to the airfield from here." Even knowing he was playing with fire, he cupped his fingers beneath her chin. "And if they're that close to kicking the bucket, I'd rather have them go on the ground than up in the air."

"You're terrible."

"And you're amazing."

When her lips parted, either in surprise or because she was planning to argue, he ducked his head and took her mouth. Softly at first, just a brush of his lips against hers, teasing his way from one corner to the other.

Hooyah. She didn't pull away. Instead, she grabbed hold of the front of his shirt, slanted her head, and with a shimmering sigh, she softened and sank into the kiss. Because it had been too long since he'd been with any woman, and far too long since he'd been with the only one who'd ever made him ache long after she'd sneaked away like a cat burglar, he deepened the kiss, stroking his tongue against hers in a rhythm that had him remembering how it had felt to be buried deep inside her, his hands on her hips, holding her as he'd driven them both toward release.

Knowing he should leave now, while he still could, Finn slipped a hand beneath her slicker. He brushed his fingers against the strip of skin at her lower back, bared by her shirt rising as she strained toward him. It was as soft and satiny as he remembered, and as his fingertips began to burn with sensual memory, he slipped his hand down the back of her jeans. She moaned into his mouth when he cupped one butt cheek and began massaging the smooth, firm flesh.

Then, just when he was about to play the airline owner card and leave Yazz or one of the other pilots to deal with his seniors' damn bucket lists while he took her into the cabin and finished this, she pulled away. And stared up at him.

"That was a mistake," she said.

"Last night might have been a mistake," he allowed. "Today it felt pretty damn good."

"I don't do hookups." Realizing that's exactly what they'd done in San Diego, she said, "Okay, correction. I slipped once." As if belatedly realizing that her nipples were taking longer than her brain to get the message that she was throwing a flag on the play, she pulled the slicker closed. "But that was crazy chemistry."

"You're not going to get any argument from me. I did, by the way, score an A in chemistry at the Academy."

"The Academy?" Her eyes, which had been heavily lidded after that shared kiss, narrowed. "You went to Annapolis?"

"Yeah." He felt her pulling back. Not just physically but emotionally. "So what?"

"You never mentioned that."

"And you never mentioned you could cook. Conversation wasn't exactly a priority."

Nor had food been. Except for when they'd fed each other the chocolate-dipped strawberries some unseen hotel staffer had delivered to his suite while he'd been downstairs. Afterwards he'd spent a long part of the moon-spangled night spreading the accompanying whipped cream over her breasts, then licking it off.

She turned away to look out at the cobalt-blue lake. "It was just sex."

"Hot, blow-your-mind sex," he agreed. "I was walking funny for a week."

"That's a myth." She looked back toward him, her gaze drifting down to a boner that, like her nipples, hadn't yet gotten the memo that this wasn't going to go anywhere. At least today.

"Hand to God." He raised his right hand. "If I'd been an athlete, I'd been benched."

She didn't smile. "Look," she said, "this isn't really personal—"

"Funny, it felt like that a couple minutes ago."

She looked at him for a long beat. "I don't

want this."

Knowing he was being perverse—but for some reason this woman always had him behaving out of character—Finn lifted his brows. "What?"

"This." She waved a hand. "You. Me. Together... All this..."

"Chemistry."

"Exactly." That kiss they'd shared proved her to be a liar, but Finn got the meaning. Because he felt the same way. At least he thought he did. The pitiful truth was that whenever he was within kissing distance of Tori Cassidy, all his good intentions went flying right out the window.

She'd been different from the beginning. Having spent time with her the past two days, he was coming to realize exactly how different she was than his usual women. Although he still hadn't pried any of the secrets he knew her to be hiding in her past from her, Finn knew that Tori Cassidy was the kind of woman a guy settled down with. Had kids with. Built a life with.

Not that there was anything wrong with that, he considered, thinking once again of his brothers. But he wasn't that guy.

"What are you doing on the Fourth?"

"The Fourth?"

"Of July. It's the day after tomorrow."

"Oh." She looked surprised. "I guess I'll be doing what I'm going to do today. Trying to create two recipes that won't get me chopped."

"Chopped?"

"It's a cooking show. Four chefs get these baskets, and… Never mind. That's not important. I was just responding to your question."

"Alaska's as patriotic as the rest of the country," he said, forging on with the conversation even as the voice of reason in the back of his mind kept trying to remind him that the smart thing to do, if he really wanted to stay uninvolved, was to keep his distance. "But we don't do fireworks, because sunset comes at 11:59 p.m. and only lasts a couple minutes. So, mostly, it's a regular workday. But from what I've been told, Barbara Ann realized skipping the day bums out tourists, who are used to making a big deal of it, so Caribou started putting on a parade a decade or so ago."

"People like parades."

"I guess so." Finn definitely wasn't looking forward to the upcoming one. "Osprey Air always has a float." One Mary had waited to spring on him until a week ago, when it was too late to back out without pissing off both her and Barbara Ann.

"Good for them."

"And, since I'm the new guy, I have to ride on it." Something he hadn't realized when he'd made the decision to keep his ownership a secret, which kept him from appointing someone else. Or nixing the damn float in the first place.

"Yay you."

"I thought maybe you'd like to ride on it with me."

"Me?" Her slanted gypsy eyes widened. "Why?"

"Because I don't want to have to be up there alone."

"What about the other pilots?"

"They've already done their turn. It's like new guy hazing."

Her tasty lips quirked a bit at the corners. It wasn't a full-blown smile, but it had him hopeful. "I'm sorry. But I don't do floats."

"How can you know unless you try?"

"Believe me, I know."

Yet more backstory he wasn't getting. Not that he needed to know, since he was going to keep his distance.

And how's that working for you?

"Why can't you just say no?" she asked. "Pull out that alpha male 'tude you do so well."

Were it only that easy. He blew out a long breath and realized he was going to have to share something to get something. "Okay. It's personal. I owe Mary Muldoon, who runs Osprey."

"Why?"

"I told you I grew up in a big family."

"Yes, and I envy you that."

"Don't. Because we definitely weren't the Waltons. My older brothers all have different memories of that time, but for all of us, our entire lives were divided into *Before Mom Died* and *After Mom Died*."

"For you, having been four, it would be mostly after," Tori said.

Finn hated the sympathy he viewed in her gaze. "I'm not telling you this so you'll feel sorry for me."

"I didn't think you were. But I am having trouble connecting the dots between that and the woman who runs the airline who's coercing you to ride on a parade float."

"My dad apparently changed after Mom died. I don't remember him being any other way, but he threw himself into work, and we kids were pretty much left to fend for ourselves."

He paused, realizing that talking about nannies would take the conversation in a direction that wouldn't help his cause, given what she'd said about never getting involved with another rich guy.

"We had sitters." That was simply a nuanced word, he assured himself.

It's more than that, given your intent to mislead, Finn Brannigan, Sister Bartholomew piped up yet again. Damn annoying nun.

"James, being the oldest, became a surrogate

father. He'd give Dad daily reports on all our grades, sports, accidents, like running an ATV into the fishing pond and Gabe falling out of the tree house. And, since we were boys, fights.

"Dad would come up with a response, which, if positive, James would pass on. Or, just as likely, it would be left up to him to dole out punishments like grounding or taking away the car keys. Not that I was old enough to drive during that time.

"The rest of us muttered and complained a lot about him being on the top of the pedestal and receiving what we viewed as special attention. I was only ten when he went off to college, but even I could see how things fell apart even more without his hands on the reins.

"Anyway, when I was thirteen, Dad surprised the hell out of me by inviting me to go with him on his annual fishing trip up here to Alaska. I didn't have a clue why. I can't remember any of my brothers ever going off on a vacation with him, but I jumped at the chance."

"You came here?"

"Yeah. I got to see a side of him I'm not sure many people did. He acted like a regular guy."

"As opposed to…"

Once again Finn was skating on thin ice. "It's hard to explain." And wasn't that the damn truth? "I guess the best way to put it is that he mellowed out from his usual workaholic, type A personality. He seemed to actually care about me, not as one of a noisy, rowdy gang of kids he'd been left with but as an individual."

"That must have been nice."

"It was great. I liked the fishing okay, and hanging out with the other guys around the campfire at night was cool, too."

Remembering how amazed he'd been at how well his father got along with everyone, Finn understood why he'd chosen that fake name. If those various carpenters, insurance salesmen, and motorcycle mechanics had realized they were fishing with a billionaire, the entire dynamics would've changed. That thought also had him realizing that he and his dad had something in common after all. Both of them wanted to be accepted for themselves. Not as an extension of the world-famous Brannigan brand.

"But it was Mary's husband, Mike, taking us flying that made the trip for me. He let me handle the stick, which was amazing at the time. But more, it was the way they each welcomed me like I was one of their own kids. Looking back, I think Mary must have sensed how lonely I was, because she went out of her way to make me feel special. The way other kids with moms probably felt every day."

"I'm so sorry." She put a hand on his arm.

"I didn't tell you that story to get sympathy," he said. "Just so you'd understand why I can't just say no." He sighed. Heavily, and scrubbed a hand down his face. "Did I mention she wants me to wear my Navy fight suit?"

Despite the seriousness of the topic, Tori laughed. "So, you're going to be a not-very-subtle human billboard telling potential customers that Osprey Air is the best commercial airline up here because they have an actual Navy hero fighter pilot at the controls."

"Take out the hero part, and that's pretty much it," he agreed glumly.

"I'm not taking that part out. I've seen carrier landings on NCIS. Which looking amazingly difficult to do and, quite honestly, one of the only reasons I was willing to go up in that flying boxcar with you. But I'm still not going to sit on a float and wave like some parade queen." She paused a beat. "However, if you and Mary agree, I'd be willing to sing."

It would be so much easier to keep his distance if the woman wasn't so damn nice. "Mary would be over the moon. And I'd seriously owe you."

After walking her to the door, Finn caught her arms, drew her to him, and gave her what he'd intended to be a short, quick kiss but quickly escalated into a long, deep kiss that had his body humming with need.

"We have to stop doing this," she complained after they'd come up for air.

"Nothing's going to happen unless you want it to."

"I'm not sure that's all that reassuring," she admitted.

"You probably realized, when you agreed to cook at the café, that you're going to have to leave this cabin at the end of two weeks."

"Because it's tourist season," she said. "And yes, I did realize that, but I figured I'd burn that bridge when I came to it."

"I can probably help you out with that."

She narrowed her eyes. She didn't trust easily. Then again, however long she'd spent with the Covingtons had probably taught her a lot of lessons. Which brought him back to how the hell a smart, accomplished woman like her would have gotten herself mixed up with a weasel like Covington IV.

"How?"

"I'm staying down the lake."

"I'm not moving in with you."

"You wouldn't have to. There's a guest cabin next to the house I'm renting. It's empty, so you could move into it anytime you wanted."

"Why isn't it already rented?"

"It came with mine as sort of a package deal."

He was standing on the slippery slope of another of those damn lies of omission, not telling her that his father had built both the larger cabin and guesthouse he'd never used, to Finn's knowledge. Perhaps he'd been someday planning to get the entire family together up here. Maybe he was even looking forward to taking grandkids fishing. Yet another thing about the illusive Colin Brannigan Finn would never know.

His father was starting to remind him of Laura, in that old '40s film noir mystery where the detective investigating a socialite's murder fell in love with her from her portrait, letters, and diaries. Only to discover that she hadn't actually died. Which wasn't the situation in this case. Although, at the old man's demand, there hadn't been any funeral or even memorial service, he was real and truly dead.

"I'd want to pay rent."

"Says the woman so financially in the red she's willing to literally sing for her supper. And before you can argue, I'm not paying anything."

Which was true.

"Why not?"

"Because it comes with the job."

Still true. Since he'd inherited the airline and the house just happened to be part of the airline's assets, due to some sort of complex one-percenter business tax deal his father had created.

"I'll think about it," she said.

"Why don't you do that?"

He gave her another quick, hot kiss and, although it was one of the hardest things he'd ever done, walked away.

15

TORI HAD HEADED home from the Caribou Café, intending to get started planning dishes to run by Barbara Ann, but instead, some lyrics began running through her head. Since she'd learned long ago that not listening to her muse, which could be a PMS-irritated bitch if ignored, was a mistake, she picked up her Taylor, retrieved a legal pad from her suitcase, settled down in one of the leather chairs, and began plucking the strings.

> *Love is not an easy game,*
> *I always lose the final round.*
> *Home has never been a stable place,*
> *It always moves around.*

Close, she thought as she wrote the lyrics down. But not quite there. She crossed out the *is not* and changed it to *has never been* to better fit the third line. And *stable* wasn't quite what she was looking for.

After trying a few more synonyms, she settled on *certain*. Which was definitely true. There'd been nothing certain about her life since the day her parents had been killed on that narrow Maui road.

Shaking off memories that were painful, even now, she moved on to the second verse.

> *I have sailed to every distant sea,*
> *I leave love before love can leave me.*
> *It's so much easier to lose than keep,*
> *These dreams of home.*

"Feels," she murmured, crossing out three words. Sometimes what looked good on paper didn't quite work when sung. "It *feels* much easier to lose than keep."

Better. It was funny, she thought, how her feelings, which she worked so hard to keep locked up tight inside the box that was her heart, would come pouring out in her music. Also, she couldn't help noting that she hadn't written a line since agreeing to marry Carter. Somehow, this wild, beautiful place, and, although she hated to admit it, Finn, had unlocked that box, allowing her carefully held emotions to escape.

> *Carry me home,*
> *Carry me home.*

Home hadn't been a certain place for a very long time. Yet as Finn had flown them over the rivers and mountains, Tori had thought she'd heard a distant click. As if, perhaps, Denali, which she'd read in her tour guide was a sacred place to natives, had somehow struck a chord deep inside her.

She shook off the strange feeling. "This isn't the time for introspection. You have work to do. Menus to plan." It had merely been a momentary response to Finn's kiss, along with those lyrics that had risen from somewhere deep inside her, and the almost mystical mountain whose top was becoming draped in a cape of fluffy clouds.

Putting down the guitar, she turned a page on the pad and got to work.

✧ ✧ ✧

THE DAY AFTER having left Tori at the cabin, Finn had just landed in Anchorage and sent his passengers on the way back to their cruise ship when his phone vibrated. Pulling it from the pocket of his jeans, he read the name on the caller screen and braced himself for bad news.

"You've changed your mind," he guessed.

"About what?" Tori asked.

"The parade thing tomorrow."

"Oh. I haven't even thought about that. But I'll be there."

"Great." Though he wasn't all that psyched to learn that she hadn't been thinking about him as he had her.

"I'm in town. At the Trading Post."

"Okay."

"Shopping."

"That's a good place for it," he agreed.

"I'm sourcing the menu for Barbara Ann's test dinners, and they don't have everything I need."

"She said you could go as far as Anchorage," he reminded her. Then realized why she was calling. "You need me to pick up some groceries."

"Only if you have time." Although like every other male he knew, Finn had never been one to pick up on female conversational nuances. But he could hear what sounded close to panic in her voice. "And wouldn't mind."

"Sure. Give me just a minute." Not having any scrap paper, he turned the flight manifest over to the back and took out a pen. "Shoot."

"Thank you!" She exhaled a breath. Then rattled off a short list of ingredients that even he could recognize. Except one he'd vaguely heard of but never tasted.

"Port?"

"It's a fortified wine from Portugal. From the Douro Valley. It comes in a range of styles and qualities and is typically a medium-dry dessert wine. But for cooking I don't need an expensive vintage. Ruby port's the least expensive, but it'll work fine for what I'm planning."

"Which would be?"

"Braised beef short ribs on a bed of garlic mashed potatoes and sautéed kale."

"Sounds manly." And really great. Though he could do without the green stuff. "Need a taste tester?"

She paused for a moment. He could hear her thinking. "That could be a help, since you're right about it being a manly dinner. And you are, after all, a man."

"I'm glad you noticed."

She laughed that musical laugh again. When he laughed with her, a curvy redhead, dressed in the white uniform of a cruise ship captain, passed by him. She stopped long enough to give him a slow once-over. There'd been a time when he probably would have jumped on the invitation in her smile, but that had been before Tori. He gave her his best apologetic grin and shrugged as he held up the phone as proof that he was already committed.

She shrugged shoulders topped with gold-braid epaulets, gave him another, slightly regretful smile, then walked away. Because he was male, and not dead yet, he allowed himself a moment to enjoy the view of her hips sashaying down the dock, then returned to the woman who, he'd begun to fear, had slipped beneath his private barricades a long time ago.

"I'm meeting some passengers in a couple hours," he said. "That'll give me time to pick your stuff up."

"Thank you," she said again. "I know it's foolish, but I almost had an anxiety attack in the store when I realized they didn't have everything I needed. I mean, I know how to cook, and while I'm grateful to Barbara Ann for the opportunity, the Caribou Café isn't exactly the French Laundry. Which is a famous restaurant in Napa Valley, not actually a laundry."

"Then why the name?"

"The stone building was originally built as a saloon in nineteen hundred, not far from a veteran's home. But then a prohibition was passed to make selling alcohol near a veteran's home illegal, so it was sold to another couple who turned it into a steam laundry and named it the French Laundry. Then World War I, prohibition, the depression, and World War II caused the collapse of the Napa Valley wine business. Then in the seventies it was turned into a restaurant and why is any of this relevant?"

"It isn't," he admitted. "I just like listening to you talk."

Her voice dropped off like a stone tumbling off the mountain into the lake.

"You still there?" he asked finally.

"Yes… You confuse me," she said.

"Ditto, babe. And as much as I've enjoyed this, I'd better go get your port and stuff if I want to get back here to pick up my passengers."

"I owe you."

"No, you don't. But if you need any help coming up with a way you'd like to repay me, I'm more than willing to offer a few suggestions." Her smothered laugh had his heart doing a weird clutching thing. "I should be back by four. Is that enough time?"

"Plenty. Do you think you'll be able to find port there? I could change—"

"Ruby port, not the expensive stuff. Six short ribs. Leafy green stuff. No problem. Anything else?"

"If they don't have kale, Swiss chard will do. The Trading Post turned out to be surprisingly well equipped for basics."

"I'm told a lot of people save money by cooking after a day on the mountain."

"That explains the two walls of frozen dinners," she said, spicing her words with an extra spoonful of derision.

"Hey, you just happen to be talking about my staff of life."

"Breakfast at the café, frozen dinners. You're going to be easy to please."

"You've already proven that," he said.

Then hit end, leaving her to think about him. And, maybe, start planning more than just those short ribs.

16

AFTER ARRIVING BACK at Caribou with his passengers, whom he'd driven over to Barbara Ann's B and B, Finn returned to the office with his flight log. He'd already called from Anchorage to have his schedule changed. Knowing that July was going to be a busy month and having already invited himself to sample Tori's dinner, he'd decided to take some of his required weekly thirty consecutive hours off duty time tonight. He'd drop the port, ribs, and green stuff by the cabin and take a few more flights, then just let the evening unfold.

Although Mary occasionally grumbled about the "old days," when the FAA wasn't so strict, Finn knew safety was always her first concern, so she'd been quick to grant the time. Especially, as he'd pointed out, he was using some of those thirty hours to ride her damn float.

"So, I heard you and the Cassidy girl had breakfast together this morning."

"Not much gets by you," he said mildly.

"Not in this town." She tapped her pen on the desk. "You also took her rental car over to her last night."

"I did. And it's not what you think. I didn't spend the night with her."

Her brows rose above the purple frames of her reading glasses. "Did I say anything?"

"You didn't have to," he said. "It might as well have been written all over your face with an industrial-size Sharpie."

"Don't hurt her," she said, as serious as he'd ever seen her.

"I wasn't planning to."

"Oh, I know that. But I'm not blind. You recognized her name the minute you heard it."

"Maybe," he hedged.

"Absolutely. It's a good thing you were a pilot and not a SEAL like your brother, because you would've been a failure at undercover terrorist fighting stuff. You can't lie for bagels."

"It's beans."

"More like bullshit." She cocked her head and gave him a long look. Wanting to prove her wrong, that he could be just as undemonstrative as Max, he stared right back at her.

"Barbara Ann said she was afraid the electricity sparking between the two of you was going to blow all the café's fuses."

"Barbara Ann's a card-carrying romantic." Thus the cake and the damn glitter, which, since he was still brushing it off body parts, had turned out to be the herpes of the craft world.

"There is that," she said. "But that doesn't explain what you were doing buying short ribs and kale when everyone knows that you neither cook nor eat green vegetables."

"I can cook." A burger, hot dog, or even a steak, which to Finn's mind was all a guy needed to know how to fix. Not that he did it all that often when the café could serve the same thing up without leaving him any dishes to wash. "And green vegetables taste like grass."

"Which, unless you spent a previous life as a cow, you've never eaten so have nothing to compare it to."

She had him there. "How do you know I bought that stuff?" Finn had grown used to everyone knowing everyone else's business. That wasn't just small-town behavior. When pilots got together in their quarters, they could gossip like a bunch of old ladies.

"I called the market down there to order me up some frozen Gulf shrimp for my grandson Ty's sixth birthday. Don't forget, you agreed to be on the tree house building committee so he can wake up to the surprise."

"I haven't forgotten." It had brought back

good memories of being back at the ranch, hanging out in the tree house with his brothers.

"Good. Since you guys will be swinging the hammers, we women are providing the food. At any rate, I was going to have you pick the shrimp up for me since you were going to be in town anyway, but you weren't answering your phone, *as usual*."

"Geez. What's with everyone suddenly being so antsy about my damn phone?"

"Because you have the thing for a reason. So people can get hold of you."

"I answer it."

"Selectively," she shot back. With which he couldn't argue.

"Anyway, Henry Doyle told me you'd already been in and gotten some meat, wine, green stuff, and a Three Musketeers bar. The last of which is totally believable. But you could've knocked me over with a fender when he told me you'd left with that dinosaur kale."

"It's feather."

She ignored the muttered correction. "When I added that piece of information together with Barbara Ann saying that the Cassidy girl is doing a tryout to be a new cook, it all came together. You were shopping for her."

"She called and asked me to pick up some stuff while I was just waiting around for those passengers to get off their ship, so it wasn't any big deal."

"It's sweet, is what it is. I don't suppose it has anything to do with you taking your thirty hours? Like maybe she's going to be trying that recipe out on you before she sends it to Barbara Ann?"

"Maybe." Finn felt like a damn six-year-old called into the principal's office. Next he'd be scuffing his toe on the floor.

"She was engaged to be married to another man just days ago."

"I'm well aware of that," he said between set teeth.

The quirk of her lips revealed that he'd given away the fact that wasn't his favorite topic. "You didn't like the fiancé."

"He was a prick." Finn regretted the sailor talk as soon as he'd heard the word leave his mouth. "Sorry."

"Don't be. I've spent my entire adult life up here working with men. I've heard a damn sight worse. Said worse, too," Mary said. "My point was that, like I said, she's bound to be emotionally fragile right now. While you're ripe for some sheet tangling, given that you've been celibate since you arrived in town. Not for the lack of trying on the part of nearly every female under the age of fifty."

Finn figured that was an exaggeration. But not by much. "I wasn't aware my sex life was up for discussion."

"Of course it is. If you stick around long enough, you'll realize how living with the same folks day in and day out can get damn boring. We need new blood spicing up the talk."

"Happy to oblige."

"No problem. And if you decide to make a move on anyone, would you let me know? I've got fifty bucks down on Casey Doyle."

"Casey? From Midnight Sun Manicures?"

"Something wrong with redheaded manicurists?"

"Not at all. I thought she was going out with some trail guide."

"She was. Until he took a group out on an overnight trip and was seen teepee-creeping with a blond accountant from Boise." She shook her head. "You really ought to keep up with things. At any rate, she's on the market again. So, if I were you, I'd seize the carp. Before someone else lands her."

"I'll keep that in mind." For about a second. "I'm still trying to wrap my mind around the idea of people betting on who I may or may not sleep with."

"Like I said, we've got to take our entertainment where we can find it. Not that you're helping things out that much, because for a hotshot flyboy, you lead about the most unexciting life any of us have ever seen.

"Barbara Ann's holding the pot. Which is growing considerably, by the way. So, the longer you hold out, the better it'll be for me if you end up with Casey."

"What makes you think I'm the kind of sleaze guy who'd kiss and tell?"

"You wouldn't have to. Someone would find out."

And from there, the word would spread, Finn knew. He didn't mind for himself, but if things were to happen between Tori and him, he'd want to protect her from gossip. Especially if she were to stay here for longer than the season.

"One thing you are going to have to do before you get involved in any hanky-panky," she warned. "You need to tell her who you are. Because while I understand your reasons for not wanting people to know you're one of *those* Brannigans, somehow things always get out. And it's not as if you're the mogul your father was—"

"Not even close." Finn hadn't even looked at Osprey's books. Mary had told him they were running in the black, and her word was good enough for him. All he wanted to do was fly.

"I realize you only knew him as a hard, distant man," she said. "One who had to have been focused on business to build such an empire—"

"You think?"

"I don't think. I know. That man who sat around the campfire telling tall fish tales, and who took you up flying with my Mike, and who, may I point out, paid for those flying lessons you took with money he'd worked damn hard for, *that* man was Colin Brannigan, the billionaire who'd lost his parents when he was a teenager. In a plane crash," she pointed out. "Which makes it even more remarkable that he'd not only pay for all those flying lessons for you but even left you Osprey as a legacy."

Finn had heard about his father's parents, but he'd never really put the pieces together until now. "I suppose that would've been hard," he allowed. As bad as having lost his mom was, Finn guessed it would've been worse to lose both your parents at an age when your head was already messed up from teenage hormones.

If so, the old man must have gotten over the loss and moved on, because according to his older brothers, there'd been a time when their father had been all in when it came to his family.

Which, in turn, had Finn thinking about what Luke had told him about their dad having fallen in love with their mom at the lodge Luke had inherited. The one where Luke was currently building himself a new life with his old girlfriend and her niece. It still weirded him out to think of Luke settling down in one place. At least he wasn't entirely giving up his extreme video business.

When Luke and Lizzie had told him about their engagement on FaceTime, he'd learned that his dad and mom had shared a teenage summer romance that hadn't survived time and distance when Kathleen Hayes had returned home to Kentucky. But then his parents had found each other again at the lodge. Coincidentally his dad had been twenty-seven when they'd reunited. The age he was now. Which didn't have anything to do with him. It was just another coincidence.

"I'd better get going and drop off the stuff at the cabin."

"And tell her?" Mary asked pointedly.

"No time right now," he dodged the question. "Not if you want me back here for the afternoon flights."

"But you *will* tell her who you are? And that you own Osprey?"

"Sure."

Someday. But Tori was at a stressful time in her life. Why risk making things even worse? That's what Finn told himself as he drove toward the other side of the lake. By the time he'd reached the cabin, he'd managed to convince himself that it was the best way to handle the situation.

✦ ✦ ✦

WHAT HAD SHE been thinking? Barbara Ann had been right. Frying wings and grilling sliders was very different from the meals she'd planned. One using the short ribs, and to show versatility, another using fresh king salmon, which, luckily for her, was in season. The two dishes were ones she'd made before over the years. She'd tinkered with them until she honestly believed they could hold their own against any similar dishes in many of the top restaurants in the country.

While in southern Oregon for the Music in the Mountains festival, she'd taken a road trip up the coast and had dinner at Chef Maddie Durant's Michelin star restaurant in Shelter Bay. The chef had been warm, friendly, and despite the fame garnered by her time as a TV chef, eager to chat with diners. It had been the Culinary Institute of America–trained chef who'd recommended adding the port for an extra layer of depth.

But cooking for the various foster families she'd lived with, and for friends—most of whom were musicians, always happy for a free meal—was turning out to be far different than auditioning for a job. For the first time, she truly understood how those *Chopped* contestants felt. Though, in a way, they might have had it better. Because they were working against the clock and didn't have time to second-guess every ingredient.

Like she'd been doing since she'd found her-self frozen in the vegetable section of the Trading Post, torn between fresh coriander or flat-leafed parsley to add to the crushed potato/crab mixture she was planning to top with crispy grilled salmon and surround with roasted grape tomatoes.

"Perhaps you're taking too much of a chance," she worried aloud as she paced the cabin floor, watching out the window for Finn.

She'd made the potato/crab mix as a warm salad many times before but had decided topping it with the salmon would elevate it and impress Barbara Ann. "People here eat salmon and crab all the time." This was where both the seafood ingredients came from, as anyone who'd ever watched *Deadliest Catch* knew all too well.

"You should've stuck with manly meat. May-be braised pork belly over a fennel and cabbage salad." Who didn't like bacon? "Damn." She rubbed her forehead, feeling the beginnings of a major headache. "You should have had Finn pick up some pork belly while he was getting the ribs."

Even as she paced and worried, Tori knew she was behaving uncharacteristically. She'd never been a fusser. Having lived with disruption during her adolescence and teen years, she'd learned to keep her expectations low. Which was why, as upsetting as having her music stolen from her in her record company's bankruptcy had been, she hadn't been entirely surprised. Those things happened. And since she'd never be able to afford to buy her songs back, she'd just have to write new ones.

Two years ago, she'd won a gig teaching at a WomenSong summer music camp in the Ardennes, in southern Belgium, only to have it closed down after the first week because the programs coordinator and treasurer (both married to other people) had run off together. Unfortunately, they'd stopped to drain the camp's bank account before boarding their plane to Paris, stiffing the students and the staff.

Rather than cry crocodile tears, she and her Taylor had hit the road, on buses, trains, and occasionally hitching, spending the rest of the summer singing her way across the country and into France as far as Paris, where a helpful travel agent had helped her trade in her original return ticket to one back to the States.

And, of course, then there'd been that fiasco with Carter.

No. She wasn't going to think about the man who should have broken her heart. But, she'd realized, he couldn't. Because she'd never given it to him.

Deciding that all she was doing was wearing a path in the wood plank floor, she picked up her Taylor and went back to work on her new song, which was showing progress.

My foolish heart is like a gypsy wind,
A lonely ship, a skipping stone.
Tossed by lovers' lies and promises,
Fated to wander and to roam.

And hadn't she always done exactly that? And would again. Despite Barbara Ann's offer for full-time employment, Tori wasn't intending to stay in Caribou beyond the summer season. Especially not with Finn living here.

The former fighter pilot was too hot. Too tempting. Too male.

She'd no sooner sung that last word than she heard the Jeep approaching. Jumping up, she left her guitar on the couch, ran to the door, and threw it open.

"Hi." Unlike when she'd first spotted him standing like a lone beacon in the Anchorage terminal, Tori had never been so happy to see anyone. She did wish she hadn't sounded schoolgirl breathless. "You made it back."

"That's the plan," he said as he walked toward the cabin on that loose-hipped, long-legged stride that didn't help with her decision to give up men when she'd boarded that plane at LAX bound for Alaska. "Since crashing really wasn't an appealing alternative."

"I'm glad. And not just because you'd have

taken my ribs down with you."

"Nah. No way would I be responsible for you blowing your audition. After dragging myself out of the flaming wreckage, I would've somehow managed to crawl my way back to town, even though, battered and broken, I'd be fighting off the grizzlies and wolves trying to take your precious short ribs away."

Layered, she considered as he walked into the house with two green-and-black canvas bags. Finn Brannigan had more layers than that ripped-off version of a blooming onion Barbara Ann served at the café. Tori had taken the laminated dinner menu home so she knew what she'd be competing with. Every so often that aviator's ice would crack just enough to give a glimpse of the only man she'd ever met who was truly capable of breaking into her well-protected heart.

"I really appreciate this." Her purse was on the end of the entry table. When she went to get it, he caught her arm.

"I've got it."

"But—"

"You're going to be feeding me a better dinner than I've had in years. I should be paying you."

"Thank you." She was too poor to argue as he continued into the kitchen, where he placed the bags on the counter. Digging into the first one, she pulled out the ribs, wrapped in waxy white butcher's paper, and a huge bundle of pebbly dark green kale that looked as if it had been pulled straight from the earth.

The second bag held a bottle of port and another of cab.

"I figured that'd go well with the ribs," he said when she'd glanced over at him.

"It's perfect. And expensive." While at the Trading Post, she'd been tempted to put a mid-priced mass-market wine in her basket but hadn't been able to justify spending her rapidly diminishing cash.

"I figured it should live up to the meal."

She felt her lips curving. "I hope I can live up to your expectations."

"You've already done that." The sexy-as-sin smile he flashed had all her good parts forgetting she was *not* in the market for a replacement fiancé. "I took a few of my monthly required FAA hours off tonight and finish my last flight around six. If that works for you."

"That'd be perfect." The ribs would need to braise for three hours after searing. Which gave her plenty of time to plate around seven thirty. It was strange, she thought, living where the sun stayed up all day. She imagined it took some time to adjust, because if you just went by the way your body felt, you could be eating dinner at a summer midnight sunset. "And seriously, thank you."

"No problem," he said. "I like seeing you smile. And I'm really looking forward to tonight."

Her throat caught as his warming gaze lingered on her mouth. Was he talking about looking forward to more than dinner? Even knowing Finn Brannigan was trouble, reminding herself that all her relationships with men had been both shallow and fleeting, Tori found herself hoping that he was.

17

SHE'D LOOKED FRAZZLED. And surprisingly insecure, Finn decided as he flew two insurance agents who'd won some sort of sales trip with their spouses along the rivers and through the mountain passes, pointing out landmarks. Although it wasn't the same as seeing things firsthand, he'd learned a lot while doing research while deployed. Some locations he remembered from that long-ago summer; others he'd learned from Yazz and the other pilots, who all had a list of the most popular and asked-for sights.

Fortunately, although the guys talked non-stop, like other salesmen he'd met over the years, they were mostly happy talking to one another. Their wives did ask questions, and seemed genuinely interested in their answers.

His next flight was a couple celebrating their fifty-fifth anniversary. One of their daughters had gifted the wife with a charm bracelet with photos of their life over the years, and when she showed it off, Finn noticed how much the two had come to resemble each other over that more-than-half-a-century timeline. Barbara Ann would've described them as cute as a button as they encouraged one another as he'd helped them into the plane and held hands during the flight. Not, he realized, because they were nervous fliers but because they were genuinely still in love.

As he watched them walk back to the van they'd hired to drive them to and from the lake resort lodge, still hand in hand, Finn experienced a twinge in his chest and decided he shouldn't have eaten those pork rinds from the vending machine before taking off.

Although it had been a very long time since Finn had been on an actual, planned-ahead date, he did remember some of the basics. Including, if a woman cooked you dinner, you shouldn't show up empty-handed. It didn't matter that he'd bought and delivered the groceries. Or that she'd only invited him as a taste tester.

"First date?" Sheryl Lawson, the owner of Stems, one of the few businesses in town Barbara Ann didn't own, asked. Given Caribou's grape-vine, Finn suspected she knew that not only was it his first "date" with Tori but his first one period since arriving in town.

"Sort of," he mumbled, feeling like when he'd been sixteen and had bought a wristlet for his prom date.

"Some men like to go big with red roses."

"I'm willing to spend the bucks, but I'm not feeling those," Finn said.

Not that he knew much about sending women flowers, since most of his hit-and-run relationships in the past weren't the kind that required the additional effort, but since all the guys aboard ship with wives and girlfriends would line up to order roses on Valentine's Day, Finn was afraid she'd think he was sending some big "I love you" message that could end up being uncomfortable for both of them.

"Then you'll want something more casual?"

"Yeah. That sounds good."

"And nothing that looks like a bridal bouquet, given her circumstances," Sheryl mused out loud as she walked over to a cooler filled with blooms.

"You're a regular Nancy Drew." It appeared the honeymoon mountain cake fiasco had already made the rounds.

"I doubt you'd be having breakfast with one woman and dinner with another," she said. "Oh, some guys might. But ones who do usually don't care enough to come in here for flowers. Maybe because they're afraid I'd tell. But don't worry, you can consider me like a priest. And my shop as a confessional. Your purchase is strictly confidential."

"Good to know," Finn said. Since he'd had to park a block away, he doubted he could get back to the Jeep without some local spotting him.

"What do you think of these stargazer lilies? Many brides like them in a bouquet, but they don't necessarily shout wedding like the hydrangeas do."

"They're kind of formal." Not so different from the roses.

"They are that. Dahlias?" She held her hand up next to a bucket of bright flowers that reminded him of Tori's sunny laughter. But for some reason, they still didn't seem right.

"How about those?" He pointed to another group at the far end of a cooler shelf.

"Sweet peas." She nodded. "They're simple but lovely. And unexpected. Also, unlike so many flowers that have had their scent bred out of them, these are grown for the sweet and spicy scents."

Spicy and sweet fit Tori Cassidy to a T. "I'll take those."

"You have excellent taste," she said as she gathered up a mix of white, deep and light shades of purple, and a pink the color of the king salmon that were running in the rivers.

As so often happened, more since his father's death, making him a twenty-seven-year-old orphan, a distant memory stirred. He'd been sitting on the ground, carefully dropping seeds into a shallow trench his mother had scratched into the soil. She'd loved to garden, and since his brothers were often off doing things they'd insisted he couldn't keep up with, it had been a special time when he'd had their mom all to himself.

"She's going to love them," the florist broke into the memory that he realized had him smiling.

In under five minutes, she'd created the arrangement, wrapped it in green paper, and tied it with a bit of green-and-white twine. Then carefully placed it in a solid-bottom bag that had *Stems* written on the side in bold white script. Oh, yeah. Like that was going to keep him from being noticed.

Sure enough, Finn had gotten less than half a dozen steps after leaving the shop when Doug Green, who was taking a smoke break outside his hardware store, somehow managed to grin like a loon without the cigarette dropping out of his mouth. "Hot date?"

"Maybe they're for Mary's birthday," Finn shot back, feeling as if he'd been caught buying condoms for the first time. Which, along with the wristlet, he'd also stocked up on the night of that long-ago prom. Not that he'd gotten lucky enough to use one, but he'd been hopeful, and James had given him the stern "No Glove, No

Love" lecture back when he'd turned thirteen.

"Mary's birthday is on Halloween," the older man shot back. "So you can buy *her* some posies if you manage to stick around that long."

"I'll be here."

Finn knew many locals were waiting to see how long he'd last. He'd already figured out that bush pilots came and went with regularity. Maybe because of the longer hours for less pay, the battles with Mother Nature, or simply that they found themselves unsuited to living in the vast, northern wilderness. So far, it was suiting him just fine. And now, thanks to the hardware store owner, he had a short-term goal. No way was he selling out and leaving Alaska before Halloween.

Not only did he not want to miss Mary Muldoon's birthday, he had the feeling his love life wasn't the only thing residents of Caribou were betting on.

✧   ✧   ✧

DESPITE HER EARLIER attack of nerves, Tori had everything under control. At least on the dinner front. The ribs had been seared and braised, filling the cabin with a delicious aroma that could probably sell the meal on its own. A mix of Idaho and golden russet potatoes were boiling, and the kale had been washed and the stems chopped off. The wine had been opened to breathe. Not that she was all that sure it needed to, but given the cost, she felt it deserved it.

The wine had given her a twinge of guilt. Tori didn't know how much bush pilots made, but even during this busy summer season, it couldn't be anywhere near what pilots for major airlines made. Also, from what she'd gathered, once the secondary hunting tourist business slowed down, Finn wouldn't get nearly as many hours until winter released its hold on Caribou, which she knew would be later than the rest of the country.

"No one forced him to buy the good stuff," she reminded herself out loud.

Maybe whatever store he'd bought it at hadn't suggested more reasonable wine. Or maybe he'd known all along what he was doing and found her worth the extravagance.

Carter had thrown around money as if it was like that gilt and pink confetti housekeeping had blessedly cleaned up while she'd been away having breakfast with Finn. Not that he'd ever done anything to earn it himself. If anyone ever made a reality show about a guy version of Paris Hilton, Carter Covington IV would be just the guy.

Which, she was forced to admit again, had been his appeal. He was too vain, too shallow, too narcissistic to endanger her heart.

"Bygones," she said, her mind returning to the man who'd set off warning sirens from the moment he'd walked into the ballroom. It would have been impossible to miss him, even amidst all those military males in dress whites. Tall, with wide shoulders, he'd commanded attention without saying a word, and as those long legs had eaten up the floor as he approached the band-stand, he'd exuded a raw sexual energy that had caused her hormones to start ricocheting around as if they were inside a pinball machine.

He might be the best-looking man she had ever seen. And that was saying something since she'd been living in Southern California, where nearly every guy parking cars, waiting tables, or playing volleyball on the beach looked as if he'd just been cast to star in a *Baywatch* reboot.

For as hot as he'd been, and still was, the former Navy lieutenant was a good man. Years of experience had honed her ability to read people, and if she hadn't known she could trust him, she never would've broken her rule about having sex with a man she'd just met.

It was sometime during that long night that, despite a well-honed caution, she'd landed in a situation way over her head. Which was why she'd gone running for the hills as the first gold and lavender fingers of sunrise had begun slipping into the bedroom.

And speaking of bedrooms...

Finn was due in less than five minutes, and

with his having been in the Navy, she figured he'd be super-punctual. Which meant unless she wanted to greet him wearing flour-streaked jeans and a T-shirt with tasting stains, she'd better go change.

Caribou was about as far from formal as you could get. Still, deciding that this dinner had the feeling of a potential date, she pulled out a pair of dark-washed, frayed-hem skinny jeans (that, thanks to some serious engineering, did amazing things to her butt), and a short black T-shirt less likely to show any last-minute spatter stains. She'd had no reason to pack an apron when leaving Los Angeles and hadn't thought to look for one while in the Trading Post. Fortunately, at the last minute, she'd tossed in a pair of burnished gold ballet flats, not really planning to wear them. But just in case.

After slipping into the shoes, because there was no time to do anything with her hair, she bent over, brushing it over the top of her head, then fluffing it out with her hands to reclaim a bit of fullness the heat and humidity of the oven had flattened. She swished on a dash of mascara and was touching up her lipstick when she heard the wheels of the Jeep crunching down the gravel road.

Taking three deep breaths, she went and opened the door. He was standing on her porch, clad in another of those tight black T-shirts that stretched at the seams from his wide shoulders and clung to his drool-worthy ripped abs. His faded jeans cupped him in a way that had her wondering how she'd make it through dinner without ripping them off him.

Once she'd stopped drinking in the sight of that magnificent male body, she finally noticed those delicate pastel sweet peas he was holding. Which was when she let him into not only the cabin but her tumbling, spinning, crazy-out-of-control heart.

18

"IT SMELLS AMAZING in here," Finn said. Then, on impulse, bent to kiss her neck, right beneath her jaw, where he'd discovered an erogenous zone. "But you smell even better."

He felt her body soften, relax. Then, as if realizing that she was sinking into trouble, she straightened. "Thank you for the flowers. That's very sweet."

Terrific. If there was one way he didn't want her thinking of him, it was sweet. "The florist at Stems said they like to be put in cold water." He frowned. "I didn't think that you might not have a vase in here."

"I've got that covered." Her sweater lifted, revealing a strip of bare skin that caused a spike in his pulse when she reached up to take a tall, heavy beer glass from one of the open shelves. "This will be perfect."

She ran water into the glass, put the flowers into it a stem at a time, and in that way women seemed genetically able to do, had them as well arranged as the displays he'd seen in the cooler in Stems. "I've always loved sweet peas, though you don't see them very much anymore. They remind me of an English country garden. I tell myself I'm going to plant a garden one day, but I've never gotten around to trying. It's probably just as well, because it would blow the fantasy if I turned out to have a black thumb…

"Would you like some of your wine?"

"I'll take a glass." Even as he pictured Tori wearing a floaty flowered dress and wide-brimmed hat, strolling through a country garden, Finn was picking up on some vague discomfort vibes. Not knowing what to do about it, he figured he'd just be agreeable and hope she relaxed. Otherwise it was going to be a very long evening.

She'd turned on some music, and another memory hit. "I think my mother sang that all the time," Finn said.

"I wouldn't be surprised," she said. "Your name is Brannigan, after all, and *A Woman's Heart* is still the best-selling Irish album of all times. Eleanor McEvoy and Mary Black were precursors to Celtic Woman, and the songs continue to be well covered. I've sung 'Only a Woman's Heart' and 'Wall of Tears' myself."

"My mom would've liked you," he heard himself saying.

She'd paused in pouring the wine. "Because we both sing?"

"That's one reason." He shrugged, wishing he'd run the words through his brain first. The problem was, whenever he was anywhere around Tori, all the blood would flow south to his other head.

But it was more than that. She made him feel good. When he was with her, he didn't feel the pressure to live up to his older brothers or make his father proud. Not that proving himself to Colin Brannigan was an issue anymore, unless she was right about the afterlife and maybe the old man occasionally took time wheeling and dealing with angels to check out what he was up to.

Even though he hadn't been the daughter his mother had been hoping for, Finn had never doubted that she'd loved him just the way he was. He hadn't made the connection that night in San Diego, but Tori had him feeling the same way. She didn't go all fan girl groupie when she'd learned he'd been a carrier pilot. Although she'd claimed to be impressed, he figured he could have been a carpenter or even just a bartender, like everyone had thought Knox was, and it wouldn't have made a bit of difference to her.

As hot as she was, whatever they had going was more than sex. Unfortunately, the Brannigan males had never been comfortable with emotions, and Finn knew, and had always accepted, that he was the least open of all of them. Which had always suited him just fine. Until now.

While he couldn't quite figure out what he was feeling and then what the hell to do about it, Finn only knew that he wanted to do something. Like push her up against the wall, lift up that T-shirt, and taste those pert breasts that had fit so perfectly in his hands.

Then move on from there.

But then what?

Giving up on the problem for now, he returned his mind to their conversation.

"But Mom wasn't a professional or anything. She just sang because it made her happy."

"Music can do that," she said as she put on a thick-padded glove and pulled a heavy pan out of the oven. "There were times…" Her voice drifted off.

"There were times?" he coaxed as she shook her head and took the lid off the pan, filling the room with a cloud of flavor that had his mouth watering.

She'd made his tongue hang out from the start, even without the cooking, but whatever was in that pan was definitely a bonus for a guy who'd been living on the lumberjack special at the Caribou for breakfast, cellophane-wrapped deli sandwiches from the Trading Post for lunch, and frozen pizzas for dinner after he'd finished flying at midnight.

"Later," she said, shaking her head as if ridding it of some memory. "Right now I have to concentrate on reducing the sauce."

"What can I do to help?"

She glanced over, clearly surprised, giving him the impression that Covington IV had never offered. "You could set the table," she suggested.

"Sure." He might not be all that familiar with kitchen work, but he'd eaten enough meals to know where things went.

She pointed out where the dishes, bowls, glasses, placemats, napkins, and utensils were, and as he got to work while she did chef stuff, he experienced another unfamiliar feeling. It took him a while to recognize it, since he couldn't remember ever seeing it in action, but it felt, well, sort of domestic. Like a couple at the end of the workday preparing a meal together.

"I had a thought," he said as he lined up the silverware like sailors waiting on the deck for inspection.

"Oh?"

"I happen to know a guy at a record company."

"Really? Which one?"

"Pegasus." Finn braced himself for the question he knew was coming.

"That's a big place. How do you know someone from there?"

"He was up here visiting when I first arrived. I flew him around for a couple days."

And isn't that a bald face lie, Finn Brannigan?

It's for a good cause, Sister, Finn assured them both. "I was thinking maybe I could tell him about you. And what happened with your contract."

"Oh, you don't have to do that," she said quickly. Too quickly.

He shrugged. "It couldn't hurt. And hey, I'd probably be doing him a favor because you're really, really good. I just didn't want to do anything without running it by you first."

"I don't know...."

"Why don't you think about it?" he said as he adjusted the bottom of a knife to line up with spoon next to it.

"I'll do that." She hadn't agreed. But Finn could tell she was interested, so he let it drop. For now.

"This is nice," she said once she'd set the plated dinners on the table. She sounded as surprised as he was. The chemistry was still there, humming beneath the surface, but for this moment, there was an easy comfort between them.

"It is," he agreed as he topped off their wineglasses. "And if it tastes as good as it looks and smells, Barbara Ann's going to want to increase your salary."

It was better. Finn had eaten in enough high-end celebrity restaurants over the years on the rare occasion his father would invite him, or some of his brothers and he would go out to dinner together (especially if Gabe or James were paying), but this topped them all. Somehow it managed to be the meat-and-potatoes comfort food she'd promised, but she'd raised it to a level that it should come with one of those Michelin stars.

"This is freaking amazing."

"Thank you."

"No, seriously. It's the best meal I've ever had. Hands down."

She laughed at that. "Says the man who moved from a carrier mess to hash browns and frozen pizza."

Damn. There wasn't any way he could assure her that he knew the difference between mess and diner food and these ribs with the meat literally falling off them without getting into who he really was. And although he knew Mary was right about her deserving to know the truth, no way did he want to ruin the evening after she'd obviously been working for hours.

"I've eaten at a few high-end places over the years," he said mildly. "And believe me, this could hold its own in any of them."

"Thank you." Color rose in her cheeks. Finn had noticed that she didn't blush often. She was, in her own way, as guarded as him. He liked being able to get past her walls and please her in a way that had nothing to do with sex.

The conversation flowed surprisingly easy, moving from the Alaskan scenery, which both agreed was amazing, to some of the other places they'd visited. When they both agreed Italy was heaven on earth, Finn neglected to tell her that James had inherited a winery their mother hadn't lived to learn that her husband had bought as a surprise birthday gift after a visit they'd taken together there.

James had traveled to Positano to sell it but instead had fallen prey to the love bug that had swept through the family and was getting married in October after the grape harvest. Finn had promised to try to be there, and although it would still be hunting season, Mary had agreed he should attend. If for no other reason, he wanted to check out the female who'd finally managed to bring workaholic Perfect James to his knees.

She told him about her earliest days, when she'd sing at open mic nights every chance she'd gotten. How once she'd played a folk/Celtic festival in North Carolina where her stage had been set up ten feet from a tent featuring a bagpipe workshop.

"The music I play doesn't tend to get me booked into the kind of bars or clubs that end up with burly guys having brawls," she said. "But that's not to say things can't get dicey. Like when I was playing an outdoor wedding in Colorado. You haven't lived until you've had a yellow jacket fly up your dress while you're performing the wedding processional."

He laughed. "If I'd been there, I could've helped you out with that."

She tilted her head. Narrowed her eyes. "By lifting up my skirt."

"Absolutely." Finn wasn't about to deny what they both knew he'd been thinking. Because, hey, he was a guy, and she had dynamite limbs. "And while we're on the subject of weddings, why don't you tell me what, exactly, happened with yours?"

"It's a long story."

"I don't have to fly in the morning. And the parade doesn't start until ten. So, we've plenty of time." He stood up. "You can tell me while I clean up."

"You don't have to do that."

"You cooked. I'll clean. Matter settled."

"Bossy," she muttered. "And why do you even want to know about why I called it off? It doesn't have anything to do with us."

At least she'd admitted there was an *us*. "Because I've realized I'm a selfish guy where you're concerned." He picked up both their plates and carried them over to the counter next to the sink and dishwasher.

"Oh?" She took another sip of wine and eyed him a bit warily over the rim of the glass, making him wonder if Carter IV could've been one of those abusers who'd go off with jealousy if he thought another guy was looking at his woman.

"When we do go to bed again, and we will, I want it to be the two of us. I don't want some other guy in your head in the bed with us."

"You're awfully confident."

"I'm confident that what we had that night wasn't a one-time thing. And if you hadn't gotten scared and snuck away, we could have explored it deeper."

"You were leaving town, too," she reminded him. She did not deny being scared by the intensity of their connection. "And since you brought it up, if you were awake at the time, you could have stopped me."

"Got me there," he agreed. And hadn't he been regretting that ever since? He'd come to the conclusion that the reason he'd let her get away was she wasn't the only one who'd been shaken. "But that was then. And this is now. And for the time being, neither of us is going anywhere, so we might as well get it out into the open."

"Are you always this rational?"

His laugh was quick and rough. "Where you're concerned? Hell, no. Not at all. But aren't you curious where we might have ended up?"

"It wouldn't have lasted."

"You're so sure of that."

"Not to sound jaded, but yes. I am sure. And are you really going to make me talk about all this before we have sex?"

"You do sound jaded, yes, I am holding out for the reason you cooked dinner for me and not your new husband, and at least we've gotten to the point where we agree we are going to have sex."

"You already turned me down," she reminded him.

"Which you didn't remember because you were wasted," he reminded her back.

"There is that," she said. A little grumpily, he thought. Which had him fighting a smile.

"Look," he said, leaning against the counter and folding his arms. "You can't just tell me that you moved in with your parents' employers, who just happened to not only be your fiancé's parents but also got you arrested."

"Not technically arrested," she corrected. "I never should have said anything, but you're right, I was drunk. So, what really happened was they had me sent to juvie. Which was, at fifteen, just as terrifying as going to an actual jail with cells."

"What did you do? Boost the silverware?"

Hell, by trying to keep what had to be a difficult topic as light as possible, Finn realized he'd done the exact wrong thing when those remarkable dark eyes turned shiny.

"I'm sorry." Finn vaguely remembered the comfort of his mother's hugs. But after they'd lost her, the Brannigans had never been known for embracing. Or even touching. If you'd done something to earn serious recognition, you might be lucky to get a handshake from their dad. But although he felt totally at sea, he crossed the few feet between them and bent down to take her in his arms.

"No." She stiffened and shook him off. "Go do the dishes. If you're nice to me, or if I have to watch your face as I tell you, I won't be able to get through it."

She didn't say it flat out, but Finn got the impression that he might be the first person hearing whatever story he'd insisted on dragging out of her. Which now had him wondering if he should've pushed her that far. Then decided that, having gotten here, there was no turning back.

"Your call," he said. Straightening, he returned to the sink and began rinsing the plates. And waited.

"My life was perfect," she said so quietly he could hardly hear her over the running water. He did hear her long, exhaled sigh. "Until it wasn't."

19

TORI DIDN'T KNOW how they'd gotten to this place. She'd never, *ever* told anyone about her past. Over the years she'd tried to tell herself that she didn't want others to pity her. But now, as she ran a fingernail around the rim of the wineglass and tried to come up with the words to begin, she realized, fully, for the first time, that her reasons had always been because she didn't want anyone to know that there was something about her that made her unlovable. At least for the long term.

"So, I guess I told you Carter's family took me in after my parents died?"

"You did. You said they worked for the Covingtons."

A thought occurred to her. "How did you know his name is Carter?"

"It was on the manifest Mary gave me when I went to pick you up."

"Oh. Well. Like I said, I'd always had a huge crush on him. But he was away at boarding school most of the time, and whenever he'd come home, he didn't even notice I existed."

"I would've noticed."

As much as she hated even thinking about those days, Tori smiled. "You didn't see me at eleven."

"I don't need to know what you looked like, though I'll bet you were one of those little girls everyone knows is going to have to beat boys away with a stick," he said as he filled the bottom of the dishwasher. He had a system all worked out, she realized. Fitting items together like a Chinese puzzle.

"You're very good at that," she observed.

"When you have to keep all your stuff in a locker while deployed, you learn real quick to arrange stuff."

"You were an officer. An aviator. Didn't you have your own cabin?"

He laughed. A rich, deep sound that vibrated through her like a tuning fork. A sexy tuning fork, hitting all the good notes. "Carriers aren't designed for comfort. They're designed as floating, movable air bases, which make them preferable to land bases since eighty percent of the world's population lives within a hundred miles of the sea.

"Comfort isn't factored into the equation, and unless you're the captain or admiral, the odds of getting your own quarters is probably equal to winning the Powerball. I shared my first deployment with eight pilots. The last with four, which, in comparison, was like having the luxury suite on a cruise liner. The downside was it was right below the flight deck."

He started loading the top rack. "And that was a good diversion, but to get back to your story…"

"You're not going to drop this, are you?"

"Not unless it's too painful. Then, yeah, I guess I can go through the rest of my life making up my own scenarios."

"It's not that surprising, I suppose," she said. "One year, Carter came home from his freshman year of college and noticed I'd grown up."

"And you were how old?"

"Fifteen. Going on sixteen." In another nine months.

"That's still too young for a guy in college to be hitting on."

"Looking back on it, I agree. But at the time I was just so happy he was finally interested in me. In *that* way, if you know what I mean."

"Yeah. I get it."

"It didn't go anywhere," she said quickly. "Well, except for a few midnight kisses in the pool house." But she would have gone further. She'd been so needy at the time, and so in love with his privileged blond Wasp beauty, she would have given him anything and everything he wanted.

"Which stopped when his mother found out."

"Yes. Of course there was no way she was going to let her son risk his future with the orphaned girl of a servant." She laughed at that. "It sounds so Dickensian to hear it out loud."

"Yeah, it does. But wealth has its privilege."

"Tell me about it." Tori pressed her fingers against her eyes, trying to block the video of that time running like a never-ending loop in her mind. There'd be days, weeks, months when she wouldn't think of it. Then it would be back in full surround sound and high def. "She called social services and told them that I'd become unruly and promiscuous. Then, as a kicker, she told them she caught me trying to seduce Carter."

His back was to her, but as he went very, very still, Tori could see him stiffen. Neck, arms, shoulders, back. "And he didn't say anything to defend you?"

"No." She noticed that he didn't, for a moment, seem to believe Helen Covington's side of the story.

"What happened to Covington?"

"He was young himself."

"He would've been over eighteen. You weren't. Which would have made him guilty of statutory rape if the two of you *had* had sex."

"He admitted years later that he was afraid because the family's lawyer pointed out to him that if he did give into temptation, he could've ended up in prison instead of his fraternity house."

"So he let you take the fall?"

"He was afraid," she repeated.

"He also didn't show one damn iota of responsibility. Or honor."

Tori was not as surprised as she might have been at hearing him refer to what so many would consider an old-fashioned concept. "I wanted to believe he didn't believe he had any other choice at the time," she said.

"Because you were still in love with him."

"No. And looking back, it's going to sound terrible, but I accepted his proposal because he could give me something I wanted."

He turned around and looked her hard in the eye. "Not money."

"No. At the time the fact that he had money didn't have anything to do with it."

"Then what did you want? Love?"

"No. I knew, or thought, by then that Carter was too narcissistic to love anyone but himself." She drew in a deep breath. Then let it out. And wished she had shared her feelings with someone back when all this was taking place because she would've heard how unworkable what had seemed like a logical solution had sounded at the time. "It was foolish." Tori knew that now, but the knowledge didn't make her feel any better. "I wanted a family."

He scraped a hand over his short hair, clearly unable to follow her reasoning. "With a guy who didn't love you?"

"With a man who couldn't break my heart."

"Because you weren't willing to give it to him."

"Because I couldn't," she corrected. And didn't that make her sound even worse? "Maybe it's because of all the years in the revolving door of foster care, where I'd move from house to house with whatever of my things would fit in a plastic garbage bag, but I honestly don't think I have a heart to give anyone."

There. The truth of her emotional deformity was right out in the open. And now the ball was in his court. *Your play.*

20

THE IDEA OF a fifteen-year-old girl carrying her belongings from home to home—no, house to house, because they hadn't been true homes—in a black plastic garbage bag hit hard. "Are you saying you don't believe in love?"

She hesitated. "I guess I believe in it for some people," she said. "But I don't think it's for me."

"Join the club," he muttered as he added the capsule to the detergent box. Then shut the dishwasher door with more force than was necessary.

"Excuse me?" she asked quietly. He hung the dish towel on the handle and slowly turned around, feeling his heart splinter when he saw the concern in her eyes. Did she honestly think he'd blame her for what the Covingtons had done? Think less of her because, rather than surrender, she'd found a way to survive?

If there was one thing Finn knew a lot about, it was survival. Both emotional and physical. How weird was it, he wondered, that just when he was finding himself ready to open up, he'd fallen for a woman who'd had even more reason to lock away emotions?

"You write about love," he said. "And yeah, your lyrics are about the loss of love, but if you weren't at least open to the idea, you probably wouldn't let yourself go there in the first place."

It was also why she sang, he decided. Okay, so maybe the songs she'd played for that Navy crowd were songs to party to, not that different, he guessed, from what she'd sung at those early wedding receptions. But he'd bought her CDs after leaving San Diego and had spent a lot of lonely nights in his rack, listening to her sweet, clear voice through his headphones.

Her warm, vulnerable, wounded heart had reverberated in every song. Every verse. Every word. And because she'd poured so much of herself, so much *honesty* into her music, over those months, he hadn't been able to stop wondering about might-have-beens.

"Your cooking's like that," he said as the pieces of the gorgeous, complex puzzle that was Tori Cassidy began to click into place. "If I were a judge on one of those cooking shows, I'd know right away that you'd put every bit of your heart into whatever you make."

She seemed surprised he'd caught that. "I

loved cooking with my mother. Cooking and singing were the things that made me happiest. After I lost her, cooking turned more into a ploy."

"How so?"

"Because I stupidly thought that if I'd cook for whatever family I landed with, they'd realized I could do something special. *Be* someone special. And they'd want to keep me," she shot back. "But it never happened, okay?

"And damn, I hate this." She dragged a hand through her hair, which she'd worn down tonight. "I feel I should be paying you by the hour while you hand me tissues."

"I can get some from the bathroom."

"Not needed. Because I never cry." She folded her arms in a gesture he suspected was more self-protective than stubborn. "It's another thing I can't do."

Or wouldn't let herself do, Finn considered. He was deciding it might be time to call this off. She'd spent half her life constructing those barricades. Who was he to risk blowing them up in one night? But…

"You cried that night." He remembered brushing the single salty tear away with his thumb. Tasting it.

"An unconscious reaction to my second orgasm."

"Third," he corrected with a reminiscent

smile. "But who's counting?"

"Apparently you were," she said. "Tell me, Lieutenant, did you go back to your ship and carve notches into your bedpost?"

"It's called a rack," Finn said easily, grateful to see the return of her spark.

They'd gotten into some deeper, darker territory than he'd expected. And right now, all he wanted was three things. To first, beat IV to a bloody pulp, then, second, throw him into the sea to be torn apart by sharks. And to make this woman happy. Since Covington wasn't worth doing hard time for, Finn decided to concentrate on the third one.

"And no, I'm not one to carve notches. I remember all three from that night because that was the best sex I've ever had in my life."

That was no lie, but the truth, the whole truth, and nothing but the truth. Not that Finn was all that sure Sister Bartholomew would approve of the circumstances. Fortunately, the voice of his conscience remained silent.

She bit her bottom lip. Her eyes, which had reminded him of Bambi's when the fawn's mother had died, smiled ever so slightly. "Mine, too."

It was a near whisper, but Finn had no trouble hearing it.

"Maybe we should try it again," he suggested as he walked toward her. "Just to see if it was a fluke."

"It's a high bar," she said, taking the hand he'd held out to her.

"True. But I'm willing to accept the challenge."

THEY HELD HANDS as they walked into the bedroom, just as they had in his suite. For a man who'd lived in the fast lane of fighter jets, who'd first taken her with a power and speed that both of them had wanted, *needed*, tonight Finn seemed in no need to rush.

After he'd pulled back the comforter and tossed some condoms he'd come well prepared with onto the night table, she watched, fascinated, as he framed her uplifted face in his hands. Then leaned forward, closer and closer, until his mouth touched hers. Gently. Persuasively.

It was barely a whisper of a kiss, but she could feel it through every cell in her body. Lifting her arms around his neck, Tori leaned closer.

"I'm not going to fall in love with you." Finn Brannigan was a good man. He deserved the truth.

"Thanks for the warning." His lips smiled as they plucked at hers.

"Seriously." It was happening all over again. Fast or slow, it didn't matter. She was melting into him. "We don't even know each other."

"I think we do." His hand tunneled through her hair. Cupped the back of her head as he changed angles and had her trembling with anticipation. "More than you'll admit."

"It would be a mistake," she managed to say, and all the reasons this could turn out a terrible mistake began to drift away, like morning fog over the glassy lake.

"Perhaps." He drew the kiss out as he slipped a hand beneath her T-shirt, splaying his long, dark fingers against the rapidly heating skin beneath her breasts. "But it won't be the first one I've made." With clever fingers that reminded Tori how well this man knew his way around a woman's body, he dispatched with the front clasp of her bra. "And it's definitely one of the most enjoyable."

Too late, a little voice in the back of her mind warned as he brushed his fingertips over an exquisitely sensitized nipple, then the other as he took her mouth again, the kiss longer, deeper, reaching straight to the center of her well-guarded heart.

"Your skin is like silk." His palms cupped her breasts while his thumbs continued to stroke.

"It's Barbara Ann's lotion," she managed as other body parts began to heat up.

"It's you." His hands skimmed lower, unfastening the button at the waist of her jeans. *Lower. More.* This might not be love. And Finn might not be the man for ever-afters. But he was the man she wanted, *needed*, for tonight. "Only you."

She nearly wept when he finally lowered the zipper, the sound incredibly loud in a silence broken only by the hushed breeze fluttering the leaves of the quaking aspens outside the open window, the deep bass croak of a bullfrog in the lake reeds calling for a mate, and the distant lonely sound of an owl, perhaps complaining about the lack of darkness.

And their breathing, which, as he captured her mouth once again, seemed to have synced to an identical rhythm.

He trailed a finger along the low-cut waist of her panties. "Like silk," he murmured. "I've dreamed of this." His teasing touch went lower, over her mound, cupping her. "Damp silk."

"That's you," she tossed his words back at him as her heart somersaulted at the tenderness and her body shuddered at the heat.

"Be still my heart." He patted his chest, his smile slow and easy.

"Are we going to talk? Or do this?"

Tori was beginning to feel uneasy. A one-night stand with a stranger was one thing, even if it could have been, if she'd let it, a life-changing event. But they were creating a connection that went beyond wanting to need. Which was scarier even than when she'd gone through a neighborhood haunted Halloween house in the fifth grade with her girlfriends during a sleepover. That had been three months before her parents had been killed.

"I was figuring we could do both. It's been a long time, and I'm doing my best to pace myself here."

That caught her attention. Then again, there probably weren't a lot of opportunities for sex on an aircraft carrier. "How long are we talking about?" she asked as she took hold of the hem of his T-shirt. Although she experienced a tug of regret when he had to take his hand away to lift his arms so she could pull it over his head, the sight of his chest was nearly worth the sacrifice.

"Since we were together at the Del."

"But..." That cleared enough mist from her head to allow Tori to do the math. "That was a year ago."

"Give or take a few days," he agreed.

"Why?" She was the one who'd wanted to avoid any more conversation and just get to the safe sex part, but she had to know.

"There was a lack of opportunity while I was deployed," he confirmed what she'd already considered. "And it wasn't for a lack of opportunity."

Why don't you tell me something I couldn't guess for myself?

"But none of those other women were you."

He was such a good man. Such an honest man. Even as she told herself this could turn out to be a disaster, Tori could no more resist making love to him, just one more time, than she could fly to the moon.

Just when she felt as if she were sinking into quicksand, sassy, got-it-all-together girl returned to save her. "You sweet-talkin' sailor." She trailed a fingernail down his torso, over those rock-hard abs. God, how she loved the feel of him! A memory of that arrowing of crisp hair pointing to below his belt against her bare breasts set her head to spinning.

"I want you," she said as she resisted ripping at his jeans and instead began working at the buttons. Who had ever thought five-button jeans were a good idea? As good as they looked, it couldn't have been any woman as desperate to be laid as Tori was. "All of you. Now."

"You've got me." He held out his arms, inviting her to finish what she'd begun. "Now." Two more buttons to go. "For as long as you want."

"Hooyah," she said as she finally released him from the navy blue knit boxer briefs. He was everything she'd remembered. So large. So hard. So deliciously smooth beneath her fingers. And for this stolen time, he was all hers.

✧   ✧   ✧

FINN HAD NEVER known it was possible to literally ache for a woman. But he ached for Tori. From the sight of her, as he undressed her, slowly, trying to make this midnight sun last forever.

Her perfumed skin gleamed like gold dust in the shimmering light that, on a perfect summer day, turned the sky around Denali to a soft, buttery yellow. Her dark curls spread out on the down pillow like lush strands of dark silk.

He ached from the feel of her. The way her breasts seemed to have been created to fit into his hands alone. The subtle curve of her waist leading into a swell of hips, her lean legs, which opened to his stroking touch. The softening of her warm, willing body against his.

He ached from the taste of wine, of woman, of dreams once lost and now found.

As good as that night at the Del had been, this was somehow better. Finn felt the passion racing beneath her heated flesh as she trembled beneath him while emotions swept across her face and clouded her eyes. Tori was his. As he was hers. At any other time, such a powerful sense of belonging would've hit like a cluster bomb, but deciding to think about that later, Finn spread her legs farther apart, nipped each inner thigh, then, with just his mouth and tongue, brought her to a quick, fast, climax that caused her to cry out.

Her thighs were quaking, and she'd gone limp. But not for long, Finn vowed. "That's one," he said as he returned his mouth to hers, letting her taste herself on his tongue. "In a minute I'm going to need you to turn over."

"Bossy," she managed, even as she arched against his caressing touch. "What if I don't?"

"No problem." He flipped her as easily as John Black down at the Caribou could flip a flapjack. Then settled himself, knees on either side of her thighs. Brushing her hair to one side, Finn leaned down, and nuzzled her neck, drawing forth, not a complaint, but a long, shimmering sigh.

He kissed his way down her spine, then lifting her hips, he slid silkily, slowly, into her. Filling her. Claiming her.

Her breath grew quicker and her hips began to circle in a rhythm that matched his and went on and on. And on.

"Oh. My. God!" Limp, boneless, she collapsed onto her stomach.

Two.

"Stay with me, babe," he said, rolling over onto his side and drawing her close, holding her until she'd come back to wherever she'd flown. Finally, she opened her eyes, which were blurry with sexual satisfaction. Then, another of those prolonged moments of seriousness arose between them as she studied him. Looking hard and deep.

Damn. Mary was right. He should have told her the truth before they'd gone this far. But since this definitely wasn't the time, he ran his hand across her shoulders, drawing forth a throaty purr.

"Let me take care of something," he said. If only they'd been at his place, he would've been prepared for the damn condom change. "And I'll be right back."

He took care of business, which wasn't all that easy considering that his dick wasn't exactly in a state to be messed with, then returned to find her on her knees, holding up the condom she'd taken from the second package. Looking at her, all flushed and warm and delectable, Finn knew exactly how Adam must have felt when a stunningly naked Eve had shown up with that glossy red apple.

"Ahoy, Lieutenant," she greeted him, her eyes now clear and laughing. "Prepare to be boarded."

"Aye, aye, ma'am," Finn answered. After sprawling onto his back, he had to suck in his gut to maintain control as she rolled the latex down his length.

She knelt over him, as he had her, then, curling her fingers around him, holding him just where and how she wanted him, she slowly eased herself down, her body taking him in. Closing around him.

She was nearly there when she paused, her hands splayed on his chest, her eyes on his.

"You do realize you're killing me here," he managed to say through clenched teeth while his tongue felt as thick as a two-by-four.

"Really?" Proving that those smooth thighs were a helluva lot stronger than they looked, she slid down another inch. Then, dammit, stopped again.

He could finish this, Finn thought as his heels dug into the mattress. He could lift up and he'd be home.

But understanding that this was about more than sex, he focused every damn atom in his body into remaining stone still and prayed for strength while ceding control.

She touched her fingers to her lips. Then his.

Then, finally lowered herself the rest of the way.

Finn had traveled the world. He'd seen some amazing and wondrous sights that were now tucked away in his memory to revisit. But he knew that the sight of him and Tori joined—bodies, minds, hearts—would remain with him the rest of his life.

He had no idea how long that extended moment lasted. All he knew was that when she began to move, he was lost.

21

*F*INN HAD BEEN *flying over the mountains for six hours, looking for something, anything on the ground. He was beginning to wonder if he was going to have to return to the carrier without seeing any action when a piercing noise filled his cockpit, warning him that a missile had locked onto his jet.*

Years of training immediately kicked in. Since most SAMs flew a lead collision intercept course, flying to a point in the sky where they think the target will be, his only way to survive was to force it to re-compute a new intercept course.

While releasing chaff and flares to hopefully confuse it, he began a high G pull, rolling as he climbed, moving rapidly through three dimensions. Unable to keep up with the Hornet as Finn performed the roll, the SAM missed. That was the good news.

The bad news was that the highly aggressive defensive move had used up a lot of energy, bringing him down to one hundred and fifty knots and eleven thousand feet, which left him vulnerable to another missile. One which, dammit, both his wingman and the cockpit siren were warning him about.

Looking back over his shoulder, he saw a second SAM about a thousand feet away, closing hard on his tail. Unfortunately, there was no way to outrun it. Nor did he have the power to repeat the maneuver. Having lived with the knowledge that a fighter pilot didn't always leave the cockpit the way he got in, Finn reached up, pulled his ejection handle, and watched the canopy fly off.

Less than half-a-second after the rocket thrusters sent his seat flying into the air, his parachute jerked open.

And Finn jerked awake, an instant before the missile blew his jet apart.

The nightmare was a familiar one. Unlike the other times, as he took a few deep breaths to slow his heartbeat, Finn wasn't left feeling that he was about to die. As he looked down at Tori's silky dark hair spread across his chest and felt her slender legs entwined with his, he realized that the difference was that this time he was no longer alone.

✧   ✧   ✧

IT WAS DISCONCERTING, Tori decided a long time later after, together, they'd soared over their previous high orgasm bar. She had no idea how long they'd made love. How long she'd dozed after sliding into a post-sex bliss. No idea of whether she should be getting up to start her day or snuggling closer to him and falling back to sleep.

"How do people adjust?" she murmured against his chest as his fingers played in her hair. Had he been sleeping, too? "I've always had trouble with Daylight Saving Time."

"It's a gradual thing," he said. "I'm handling it better than I did when I first arrived. The longtimers say keeping regular hours helps."

"I think we've blown that," she said.

"But for the best reason," he agreed, drawing her closer. She could feel his body hardening again, which in turn caused her own to respond. Was it possible to become a sex addict? If it was, she had no intention of going through any twelve-step program.

"It must be difficult, flying at midnight, then starting all over again a few hours later."

"Since blue light is the most disruptive, wearing shades helps. And Mary sets the schedules to help keep her pilots' circadian rhythms somewhat in tune. But all the melatonin does result in shorter sleep cycles. I've heard about hypomania, where people can go days without sleeping, but haven't experienced it myself."

He glanced past her at the clock on the table.

"Speaking of which, as much as I hate to bring it up, I probably need to leave."

"Really?" After messing things up in San Diego, Tori was hoping to be able to spend an entire night together. Even if they only spent the rest of it sleeping.

"The flight path from the mountain to the airport is over this cabin," he said. "As you've already pointed out, my Jeep stands out."

Tori wanted not to care who knew she'd spent the night with Finn. But years of wanting to fit in, to get along, had her realizing he had a point. She'd yet to meet anyone but Barbara Ann, John Black, whom she'd be cooking with at the café, and Nancy Martin, the friendly owner of the Trading Post. She wanted people in Caribou to judge her by her cooking and singing. And her behavior. And sleeping with a guy it appeared she'd just met might make her, to some minds, appear a bit slutty.

"I hate that you have a point," she muttered.

"You're not alone." He cupped her chin in his fingers and gave her a kiss that started out all soft and feathery before turning almost instantly hot. "You know I want to stay."

"I do." The proof was in both his warm gaze and pressing against her stomach. "Maybe," she suggested, "next time we could go over to your place. Then your Jeep would be where it belongs.

And so would my rental, parked here."

Oddly, he went still. And a shutter, like the blackout drapes neither one of them had bothered to pull down over the windows, lowered over his eyes.

He'd gone somewhere. Thinking about something she couldn't discern. She placed a kiss on his cheek. "Finn?"

He blinked. "Sorry," he said. "I spaced out for a second." He rubbed his forehead, seeming uncomfortable. His erection, which had been tempting her to go for a new record, had deflated. But then he flashed her that cocky naval aviator smile Tori had no doubt had caused panties to drop over several continents, and the moment passed. "I just thought of something I have to do before the parade. Some log files I promised Mary."

"Okay." As much as she wanted him to stay, Tori didn't want to cause him to get in trouble with his boss. Feeling oddly self-conscious, which was ridiculous since there wasn't any part of her body he hadn't seen, touched, or tasted, she pulled the love-rumpled sheet up over her breasts, tucking it under her arms. "You'd better go."

"I'll be back at quarter till ten to pick you up for the parade," he said as he got out of bed and began to get dressed. "If you're sure you still want to do it."

"Of course I do." She'd given her word. "Meanwhile, I think I'll catch up on my sleep."

"Good idea." Was it her imagination, or did he sound relieved? He bent and brushed his lips over hers for what she could tell was a last kiss. "See you later."

"Later," she murmured. Pressing a finger against her too-soon-abandoned lips, she watched him leave the bedroom. Then heard the cabin door open and close. A chirp revealed he'd unlocked the Jeep's door. A moment later, she heard him driving away.

She sat there, feeling as alone as she ever had. If she'd been back in California, at least she'd have her roommate to talk with. She'd only been here a couple days and was already missing girl talk.

"You're in Alaska. Not the dark side of the moon," Tori reminded herself. She retrieved her phone and texted Zoe back in L.A.

Remember that guy I told you about in S.D.? She hit send, then waited.

A response came flashing back. No surprise there, since the rocker was never more than seconds away from her phone. Hot Navy pilot?

Yes. Him. She sent it, then waited a dramatic-pause moment. I slept with him.

I know. You told me.

No. Last night. And maybe into this morning.

She still wasn't sure what with the unrelenting sunlight and the possibility of the dialed-up-to-eleven sex having exploded her brain.

I need deets. Calling now.

A second later, her phone rang.

"Did you decide to go to San Diego instead of Alaska without telling your best friend, who was supposed to be your maid of honor?"

"No, I'm in Caribou."

"What the hell is *he* doing up there?"

"Flying. But not for the Navy. For a local airline."

"Did he follow you?"

"No. He was already here."

"Wow." Tori could hear Zoe processing that. "What a coincidence."

"There's more. He's the pilot Carter hired to fly us from Anchorage to the cabin."

"Shut up!"

"Truth."

"Okay. That's it."

"What's it?"

"He's obviously destined to be your soul mate." Her former roommate and best friend definitely went against stereotype. The redhead, who had two full tattooed sleeves, multiple piercings, who played down-and-dirty goth metal rock, had the heart of an herbal-tea-drinking New Ager who'd never met an alternative belief she couldn't embrace.

"I think you may be reading a bit too much into it," Tori suggested. "If we'd been destined to be soul mates, we would have connected the first time."

"From what you told me, you *did* connect. Enough that you got scared and ran away." Tori heard the unmistakable clicking of a computer keyboard. "Obviously, your stars were totally aligned that night. What's his name again?"

"Finn Brannigan. And what are you doing?"

"Googling him to see his birthdate. So I can do your charts."

Why hadn't she done that? Tori asked herself. Not for the star-charting thing, which she didn't believe in. But just to find out more about him. Because, she answered her own question, she'd committed to Carter and hadn't planned to look back.

"This is strange," Zoe murmured. More clicking.

"What?"

"He only has a paragraph."

"Why would he have more? He's not famous or anything."

"True. But most people have Facebook pages or are on Twitter or blog or something. All this says is that he's a lieutenant in the Navy."

"Not anymore. At least not active."

"Wikipedia isn't known for its instant updates unless they're celebrities or politicians... He attended the Naval Academy."

"I know. He told me."

"Let me cross-reference that with his name." *Click, click, click.* "Oh, wow."

"What?"

"He's like a god in those graduation whites."

"Tell me about it," Tori said on a long sigh.

"I cannot believe you ran out of that hotel room and left him on the market. If I liked guys, I'd have immediately scooped him up like a pint of Ben and Jerry's Salted Caramel Core... So, what's wrong with him?"

"Nothing."

"Tori." She could hear the familiar frustrated sigh in Zoe's voice. "Men like this do not stay on the market at...doing the math here...twenty-seven."

"That's still young." Two years younger than she was, not that she was going to allow that small difference to matter.

"For mortal men. Not for gods. Is he over-the-top kinky? Does he have a Red Room? Did he strip you, tie you up, and flog you?"

"No." They had, however, stripped each other. And she wouldn't have minded if he'd tied her up. Just a little.

"There's something wrong with him. Are you

sure he didn't throw off any serial killer vibes?"

Going against her inner Earth Mother, Zoe was also addicted to *Dateline* and *Criminal Minds*.

"None. He flies senior citizens over Mt. Denali."

"There's a lot of wilderness up there where a killer could hide bodies. You might not find them until the last glacier melts."

"He's not kinky. He's not a serial killer. He's a very nice man from a family of seven children."

"Like *Sister Wives*?" Reality TV was another of her addictions.

"No." It was Tori's turn to blow out a frustrated breath. "He had one mother. She died when he was four. He's the youngest."

"Aaah."

"What now?"

"He's obviously suffering separation issues. In that respect, you're perfectly matched. Although," she mused, "it could be difficult for one of you to make the move to forever after."

"You're jumping ahead of things," Tori complained. "We spent one night together a year ago. This is my fourth day in Caribou. I'm not even thinking about ever afters."

"Good. Don't. Because if you do, you'll fall into running mode. And if he's really as good as you say, he's a keeper."

"It's too early."

"Just saying," Zoe said. "Think about it. Seriously."

"I will. Right now I have to go get ready for a parade. I got roped into riding on a float."

"You did not!"

"Yeah. I did."

"But you don't do floats. You don't even do parades. I've never been able to get you to go to the Rose Parade with me."

"Because I don't want to camp out all night on the sidewalk."

"No. Because Brooke Wingate, who told everyone at school that you'd tried to seduce Carter when he was home for summer vacation, was a Rose Parade Princess."

"There was that," Tori admitted.

"And thus the irony of her having turned out to be Carter's mistress."

Tori so didn't want to relive that revelation.

"I've really got to go," she said. "I'm singing and I need to warm up."

"Sounds as if hot pilot god has already done that," Zoe said with a laugh. "Make sure you keep me updated." Her tone turned serious. "I don't want to quit you, Tori Cassidy. You may not be into forever afters. But you'll always be my BFF."

And didn't that cause a lump to rise in her throat? "Ditto," Tori said before ending the call.

✧   ✧   ✧

"FINN AND TORI had dinner together last night," Mary told Barbara Ann the next morning as the two of them sat in a corner booth at the café. "He was supposedly taste testing one of the meals she's making for you."

"Oh, I could tell they had a connection. Did he stay over?"

"I don't know. I suspect he wouldn't because he'd be afraid that Yazz, Jackie, or one of the other pilots might spot his Jeep."

"It does tend to stand out," Barbara Ann allowed. "Like its owner. I wonder if he told her."

"I advised him to. But he's awfully hardheaded."

"I get why he wants to keep who he is a secret," Barbara Ann said. "For the same reason his father did. So he won't be judged by some stereotype of a billionaire."

"Which Finn isn't."

"You know that. And I know that. But people get ideas into their heads and will make up their own stories. There's also the fact that while Finn's not as tall and, well, sturdy, as Colin, he has his father's eyes."

"And the identical bearing," Mary agreed. "That I-can-handle-any-damn-thing-you-throw-at-me vibe. My Mike had it, too." Her expression softened at the thought of her late husband.

"Speaking of that," Barbara Ann said, leaning

forward to make sure they weren't overheard by the server refilling coffee mugs two tables over. "Have *you* told *him*?"

"Not yet." Mary sighed and set the fork of salmon, cream cheese, and chive omelet back on her plate. "I was waiting for him to settle in." She shook her head. "That's not exactly true... You know, I shouldn't have to be the one. Colin should have taken care of that if he was going to leave him Osprey."

"True. But he didn't. And someone has to."

"Which leaves it to me."

Barbara Ann reached across the table and patted Mary's hand. "You'll handle it," she assured her decades-long friend. "But, speaking as your best friend, I will warn you that both you and the boy are running out of time. Doug Green's already figured it out. Not about Mike's connection, but that Colin was Finn's father."

Mary's eyes widened behind the lenses of today's red harlequin glasses. "How?"

"Remember when that fire gutted his hardware store?"

"Of course. I'm not senile yet and it was only five years ago."

"Did you ever wonder how Doug got the money to rebuild and restock when he'd forgotten to make his insurance payment since the fire happened while his wife was busy dying in the hospital down in Anchorage?"

"He came into some money." Having been busy organizing the wake and funeral for the grief-stricken man, Mary hadn't really given the matter any thought, other than to experience relief when he hadn't lost his livelihood along with his wife of forty years.

"From Colin Brannigan's lawyer."

"Really?" That wasn't as much a surprise as it could be, since Colin had floated the loan to help Mike and her pay for one of the Cessnas several years ago when the airline was wanting to expand. Then he'd bought Osprey after Mike's death, supporting the business financially while leaving the running of it in her hands. Which his son continued to do, which Mary could understand. Finn was like Mike. Being happiest in the air, he was only interested in the flying part of the business.

"Really," Barbara Ann confirmed. "The money came from out of the blue, and Doug couldn't figure out why until his daughter showed him how to Google Colin Brannigan, and there, all over the Internet, was a picture of none other than—"

"The man who'd come up here every year calling himself Colin Hayes."

"Yep."

"You'd think Doug would've been bursting to

tell everyone that he'd been salmon fishing with a billionaire."

"He probably would've. But the money came with a nondisclosure agreement."

"Yet he disclosed it to you."

Barbara Ann's bold, hearty laugh had total strangers in the café automatically smiling along with her. "Honey, everyone tells me everything. Why, if I ever write my memoirs, it'd probably be a best seller. Maybe even get a movie made on Lifetime."

Her expression turned serious. "And I never tell anyone anything, but I decided to make an exception in this case because you're my best friend and it involves you. Doug needed me to notarize the form for him, which is when he told me. But last night, at the Gold Gulch, he mentioned, with this really sly look, how Finn Brannigan sure reminded him of someone."

"So he knows." Mary's heart sunk at the prospect of the truth coming out before Finn had dealt with it. And she wasn't one to speak, having her own secret she hadn't gotten up the nerve to share.

"He'd have to," Barbara Ann said.

Mary stabbed the omelet with renewed resolve. "I'll try to talk with him before the parade."

22

WHILE CARIBOU MIGHT not have fireworks, that didn't mean the town totally ignored Independence Day. People began lining First Street for the parade an hour before the ten a.m. start time. At least two dozen street vendors, many of whom Tori suspected had come from nearby towns, were on hand selling souvenirs, knick-knacks, and noisemakers. The Gold Gulch had a booth selling bison sliders; the café was pushing a heart-clogging sausage, egg, and cheese breakfast sandwich between two Belgian waffles with maple syrup dipping sauce; and Mountain Munchies was offering flaky croissants and a variety of muffins.

Tori stopped by the bakery booth to thank Kendra Graham for the mountain cake.

"I'm so sorry about that." The pretty blond blushed. "The timing had to be terrible."

"It sucked," Tori agreed. She'd already realized that unless she wanted to spend the next two weeks hidden away in her honeymoon cabin, which wasn't an option, she was going to have to live with others knowing about what, more and more, didn't feel as painful as it should have. "But the cake was wonderful."

"Thank you." Relief flooded over the baker's face. "I was an art student before I turned to baking when I realized that—duh—more people buy cookies than paintings. I've just recently gotten into airbrushing scenic cakes."

"I never would have known you hadn't been doing it for years," Tori said honestly. "It so looked like the light and shadows on Denali. And the little marzipan hiker bride and groom were the perfect finishing touch."

"What did you do with the groom?"

"Bit his head off." Tori still couldn't remember having done that, but the proof was right there amidst all the crumbs, confetti, and glitter on the table the next morning.

Tori grinned, Kendra laughed with open relief, and the moment passed. If she were going to stay in Caribou, they'd probably become friends, Tori thought, as she walked away with a wax-paper-wrapped croissant. Except for Zoe, she'd never stayed anywhere long enough to make more than the most casual of friends.

While it wasn't the Rose Parade, Caribou had managed to pull together a dozen floats. Along with Osprey Air, the united borough school district, and other businesses, the Caribou Volunteer Fire Department, American Legion, and the national park were represented.

Barbara Ann, not being one to miss an opportunity, had stapled a sign to the float announcing that Tori Cassidy would be appearing live at the Gold Gulch. Beneath that, she'd signed, *Barbara Ann Carter, Mayor*. A second line read, *Don't forget to vote in November!*

"Does campaigning start that early?" Tori asked Finn as he helped her up onto the platform where they'd be sitting side by side. Mary had been right, she decided. He looked damn sexy in his flight suit. A hot, don't-worry-I've-got-this alpha male you could totally trust with your life.

"Yazz, he's another one of the pilots, told me there's no need to campaign since no one's run against her since sometime in the '80s. I'm told she's so good at the job no one else wants it, and by putting that sign up every year, she blocks any wannabes from thinking it might be a good idea to try to unseat her.

"I sure wouldn't try."

"Says the woman who had the balls to negotiate with her."

Tori liked the admiring look he slanted her when one of the parade crew miked her up. Carter had always taken her singing as more a hobby than a true career. He'd even told her that perhaps that debacle with her record company being taken over, which had put her contract in limbo, could be a good thing. Because now she'd have more time to live up to her social obligations that were part and parcel of being a Covington.

What *had* she been thinking?

She obviously hadn't been.

Surprisingly, she enjoyed the parade. It seemed as if all the residents of the town had shown up, along with those staying at the park lodges and cabins and outlying areas. Everyone was there to have a great time, shouting out to her and cheering as the float rumbled by. The song list she'd come up with was a variety of her own songs along with popular standards like "American the Beautiful," "It's a Grand Old Flag," and "Yankee Doodle Dandy." When she ended with the Alaskan anthem, all the residents sang along, cheering loudly at the last line: "The simple flag of the Last Frontier."

Afterwards, people came up to meet her, many wanting her autograph. One older man, who introduced himself as the owner of the hardware store, asked, "Do you fish, missy?"

"I've never tried," she responded.

He shot a look at Finn, who was standing next to her. "If you're going to stick around awhile, you ought to get this guy to teach you. He's done some fishing back in the day."

"I'll think about that." She smiled politely as she wondered if fishing involved touching worms.

"You do that. We carry tackle and bait, even some flies, down at the store." His gaze locked with Finn again in what seemed some sort of male contest. But a mother and daughter came out together, the adolescent girl asking for Tori to autograph her CD, and the moment was forgotten.

"Thank you," she said as Finn drove her back to the cabin. It was still a workday for him, since many of those who'd come to town had booked sightseeing flights. "I would've hated to miss that."

"Me, too," he said, sounding as surprised as she'd been. "I guess that's another thing we've got in common. Along with all that animal magnetism."

"Now you make us sound like bears or something. But I can't argue it," she admitted. "What else?"

"We're both rovers. Me in the Navy, you with your career. While those who've come up here and settled into the town seem to have found their place. Set down roots."

"Roots can tie you down."

"They can also grow things. Like a new life."

"Sounds as if you're staying," she said.

He smiled, but his eyes were thoughtful. "Like

I said, ask me again midwinter... Meanwhile, how about a late dinner at the café?"

"It'll probably be packed with all the tourists come to town. Why don't I cook you a salmon dinner? I still have another recipe I need to have perfect for Barbara Ann."

"Does it come with you for dessert?" he asked as he pulled up in front of the cabin.

She shot him a sassy look. "It could. If you play your cards right."

"You're on." He cut the engine, leaned over, cupped the back of her head, and kissed her. It wasn't long. Or deep. But it still carried a dynamite punch. "I'll call you when I look at my schedule, and we'll nail down a time."

"You're on."

✧   ✧   ✧

AFTER LEAVING THE cabin, Finn pulled off the road into a turnout and, scrolling through the phone menu, called Knox, who'd settled down with his yoga girl in a small town on the Central California coast.

"Hey, dude," Knox answered right away with the surf lingo it turned out he'd used to conceal the successful entrepreneur hiding beneath his surfer/bartender exterior. "What's the problem?"

"Why should I have a problem? Can't a guy call his brother just to talk? Did I interrupt you saluting the sun or something?"

"That was earlier this morning. Which, FYI, can be done without leaving the bed."

"TMI, dude," Finn shot back. Along with having taught him how to surf, Knox could've given graduate-level classes in cruising through a life of hit-and-run relationships. Now, from that phone call Finn had gotten awhile back, it was clear he'd become a one-woman guy.

"You called to chat?" Finn could hear Knox's eyebrow arch. "You never even respond to the Brannigan email chain."

"Maybe because no one ever sends any emails. And can you be serious for just one damn minute?"

There was a pause. "O-kay," the brother closest in age to him, the former world champion of pickup lines, said slowly. "Shoot."

"I need to know how you knew."

"Knew what?"

"That of all the women you went through, Erin was *the one*."

There was another longer pause. Then, Knox burst into a loud, boisterous laugh that Finn probably could've heard all the way up here in Alaska without the phone.

"I'm so pleased to have amused you," he said between gritted teeth. Damn, he should've called Luke.

"Sorry." He could hear his brother nearly choking as he tried to cut the laugh off. "It's just that when I found myself falling into quicksand, I called Luke to ask him the same thing."

Yeah. He could've shortcut this conversation with a call to Luke and gotten the advice firsthand. "What did he say?"

"That I should grab love where I found it. And trust my instincts...

"Look," he said into the silence as Finn tried to deal with the idea that what he was feeling for Tori, had felt from that first night at the Del, might actually be love. "The Navy wouldn't have given you those multimillion-dollar jets to play with if the brass hadn't believed in your judgment."

"I wasn't exactly playing." Finn reminded himself that only James knew about his near-death incidents, so he couldn't exactly blame Knox, who probably still thought of him as the reckless fifteen-year-old kid who'd buzzed the tree house in a rented Cessna.

"Point taken. But you need to give yourself the same credit for good judgement as the U.S. Navy did."

"I'll think about it," Finn said.

"You do that. And hey, what's her name?"

"Tori." Just saying her name had him smiling.

"Nice." Finn heard a woman's voice talking in

the background. "Erin wants to know what she does."

"She sings."

"Like Mom did."

"Yeah. But professionally."

"Cool." More murmurs. "So…" He could hear the growing distraction in Knox's voice. "Ah, you okay now?"

Finn wasn't jealous that his brothers were all having regular and probably frequent sex. The hell he wasn't.

"Yeah. I'm cool. And tell your yoga girl hi for me."

"I'll do that."

The call ended abruptly. Slamming his mind shut against any images of Knox and his woman all twisted up together like a pretzel, Finn pushed the Jeep's ignition button and continued on to the airfield.

23

THE SALMON HAD turned out as well as Tori had imagined when she'd come up with the dish. As good as it had been, the lovemaking afterwards had been even better.

The following day, she was holding her breath while Barbara Ann was sampling the dishes in the kitchen before service. Although they'd hopefully be on the menu, tonight they were being used as the "family meal" before the restaurant opened, which allowed not only the café owner but the two line cooks, the bartender from the Gold Gulch, the servers and waitresses—dressed in saloon girl outfits from the tavern—and even the dishwasher to weigh in.

"You've nailed it, darlin'," Barbara Ann declared as she glanced around at the empty plates. "These are going to sell like hotcakes. And might even get us a food critic from down in Anchorage or even the lower forty-eight to write us up."

As if having waited for her to weigh in, the

others actually applauded.

She hadn't planned to combine cooking with singing. But Tori found that she enjoyed the camaraderie of the kitchen. She'd incorporated her two meals into the Caribou's menu, and, with the owner's permission, made a few changes in others. Like adding a red wine/balsamic reduction sauce to the plate-sized rib eyes, stuffing the fresh trout with lump crab before grilling, and adding a smoked salmon/goat cheese/capers pizza that proved so popular Barbara Ann added it to the Gold Gulch's bar menu.

Even better than the compliments her food received was having Finn drop in at the end of a long day's flying, or during a break, for dinner. It was almost as if she were cooking solely for him.

She'd been nervous the first time she'd sung for him in the tavern. Although he'd told her he'd listened to her songs while deployed, it was different having him sit on that barstool, his golden eyes not leaving her for a moment. When he looked at her that way, everything and everyone seemed to fade away, like ghosts into the mist, and they could have been the only two people in the room. Afterwards, she could tell others had noticed from the knowing smiles when they'd leave together.

"We've cost Mary some bucks," he said on her one-week anniversary in Caribou. During that time, along with cooking and her gigs at the Gulch, she'd been writing more in the past days than she'd managed in months. While the wide-open spaces of the Alaskan wilderness had expanded her creativity, the real inspiration had come from making love with Finn. Tori had thought that if she could only keep him tied to her bed, she'd probably finish an entire album before her cabin rental ran out.

"How? Am I taking too much time away from your flying?"

"No. During these months we tend to push against the FAA rules, so as much as I'd love to spend all my time in bed, I'm only taking as many hours as the government requires. Some airlines ignore those limits during the season, thinking we're so far away no one's going to care."

"People who might be on a plane that crashes due to an exhausted pilot's error would undoubtedly feel a great deal different," she said.

"True. There are times, in war, when you don't have any choice but to stretch human limitations. But giving visitors memories they'll never forget, or even flying someone to go shopping for school supplies in Anchorage, isn't anywhere like war.

"But getting back to Mary, we cost her winning the dating pool."

"There was a dating pool? On us?"

"Technically on me. I didn't know it until recently. Mary had me hooking up with Casey Doyle."

"The redhead from Midnight Sun Manicures?" Tori held out a hand, taking in the nails that had been recently repainted at the shop in a summery turquoise. "Were you going out with her?"

"No. Although she's a nice woman, I wasn't involved with anyone until you came to town. Thus the size of the jackpot in the pool."

"Oh." She thought about that for a moment. "Is that what we're doing? Hooking up?"

"Maybe that's what it started out as in San Diego," he allowed, "but I think we both know that we've gone beyond that."

They had. But later, as she lay wrapped in his arms in bed, after he'd proven yet again that it was, indeed, possible to fly without a plane, Tori wondered where, exactly, they went from here.

Nothing stayed the same, she reminded herself. Which was why she could be rapidly approaching the time for her to leave love. Before it left her.

✧   ✧   ✧

AND YET SHE stayed, spending every free moment she could with Finn. After he'd stretched out her new boots, they'd gone hiking on the mountain trails, through meadows of wildflowers, along rushing water, and one day she'd stood on a glacier while he'd taken her picture, her hands outstretched, as if saluting the sun that continued to shine overhead. Even as she'd added it to her phone album, Tori knew she'd never need the photo to remind her of that perfect moment.

She'd sat on a rock, watched bald eagles soaring overhead, caught a salmon, and paddled a wooden canoe past a pair of swans being followed by their fuzzy cygnets on the lake. On a midnight sunset flight with Finn in one of Osprey's Cessnas, she'd been awed as the alpenglow gleamed a fiery red on the horizon, turning the snow-capped mountains and clouds from a dark rose to pink and, finally, a brilliant gold before fading away ten minutes after it had appeared.

She'd turned to him. "That's the most stunningly beautiful thing I've ever seen," she said. "Thank you for sharing it with me."

"I've been waiting to show it to you since that first night," he admitted.

"The night of the cake." Tori thought it said something about Finn that she could smile at that night she could still not entirely remember. "When I tried to seduce you and you turned me down."

"And have been working to make up for ever since."

"You definitely have done that," she agreed.

The next morning, on a double-dog dare, Tori dove off the end of the dock into the purest blue water she'd ever seen. The initial shock of hitting the sixty-degree water made her scream, but Finn, who dove in after her, held her close and definitely warmed her up as they treaded water. Afterwards she'd heated up even more as they'd tangled the sheets of the log-framed bed.

And every day she sang, joining the chorus of songbirds filling the summer air. There were times, when everything seemed so perfect, so idyllic, that she allowed herself to wonder if this could really be her life. When she dared to think that just possibly this time with Finn could be different. That it could actually last.

On her tenth day in Caribou, she made a bowl of tortellini salad to take to a tree house building party at the sprawling log-and-stone home of Mary Muldoon, the owner of Osprey Air. Mary, who Finn had told her was also Barbara Ann's longtime best friend, was a short, sturdily built woman with long, silver-streaked black hair and dark brown eyes. Like Barbara Ann had that first day at the Caribou, she greeted Tori with a hug.

"I've been meaning to get down to the Gulch to hear you sing," she said. "But business has kept me busier than a one-armed pole jumper."

She gave Finn an odd, hard look before taking hold of Tori's arm and leading her through the crowd of children chasing each other around the lawn, past some barbeques, where older men were drinking beer while grilling a mix of meats and huge Gulf shrimp, to a long wooden table where a group of women were seated at the end, sipping on lemonade and iced tea. If the women had been wearing flowered dresses instead of khaki shorts, jeans, and a variety of bright tops, she could have been at a summer barbecue in Savannah or Charleston.

Mary introduced everyone, many of whom turned out to be relations in some way, finishing up with a young woman with rain-straight black hair and melted-chocolate-brown eyes, who looked to be about six months pregnant.

"This is Meggie Greenlaw, my middle daughter," Mary said. "It's her boy, my grandson Ty, the guys are building the tree house for. Tomorrow's his sixth birthday. He's off at my sister Molly's place over in Healy for the night so we can surprise him in the morning."

"That's very sweet," Tori said, feeling an all-too-familiar tug of loss. She might have been an only child, so the odds of her having as big a family as this, or Finn's, could have been slim. But she wished that her parents had stayed alive to see her married. And wouldn't they have loved being grandparents?

"My husband and I were at the Gulch the other night when you sang," Meggie said. Her warm smile was a replica of her mother's. "You're very good."

"Thank you."

"Are you working on anything new?" another woman—who'd been introduced as a second cousin on Mary's late husband Mike's side—asked.

"A few things," Tori said. She'd stalled on the song she'd started when she'd first arrived, but others had been flowing well.

"It's not as if you don't have any inspiration," an older woman, who looked to be somewhere between eighty and a hundred, said. Tori couldn't remember exactly her relation to Mary, but from the way she sat like a queen at the end of the table, her snow-white hair braided in a coronet around the top of her head, it was obvious that she was the family matriarch.

Her still-bright gaze moved to the far side of the lawn, where the men were busy with saws, hammers, and drills. Finn was on the top of the tree house, straddling the top ridge as he wielded a drill setting screws into the metal roof panels.

"Nothing quite like a man in a tool belt," Meggie said with a sigh. "My Dennis can catch fish like there's no tomorrow, but he's all thumbs when it comes to being a handyman."

"Looks like he's handy enough," a fifty-something woman said. "Given this is going to be your fourth in ten years."

The blush rose all the way to the roots of Meggie's dark hair. "I'm not going to deny that," she said. "But I've told him, this is the last one. After she's born, he's getting snipped."

"I'll bet that conversation went over like a lead pontoon," Mary suggested.

"It wasn't the easiest," Meggie allowed. "But he eventually saw the light."

"That Finn reminds me a lot of Mike," the oldest of the group, who'd pointed him out, mused.

"Mike was real handy with his tools," Mary agreed. "So, Tori, is this bowl of salad something you're thinking of adding to the Caribou's menu?"

The conversation shifted to food, which in turn led to memories of past gatherings, which led to conversations and stories of family members lost over the years. Once the tree house was done, the men joined the group, changing the topics to tall fish tales, sports, and whether or not the Alaska Aces hockey team would win the champion Kelly Cup for the fourth time in franchise history.

Finn was a *cheechako*, which Tori had learned

was native for newcomer, but it was obvious that he'd already fit into this community. Watching him flatter the women, talk good-natured smack with the men, and be patient and easy with all the children, Tori could see that he was a good man. Hardworking, honest, the type of man she could possibly build a life with. And wasn't that too, too tempting?

24

A SUMMER STORM came barreling though the
mountains that night, bringing with it
rumbling thunder, flashing bolts of lightning, and
torrential rain that lashed at the windows.

"I'm glad we're not camping out in that,"
Tori said as she snuggled close with Finn beneath
the covers. Since storms had always made her
edgy, she knew better than to try to sleep, so she'd
opened the blackout drapes and watched the
clouds, which had darkened the usually bright
sky. A deafening crash of thunder had her moving
even closer and holding on tight.

"They say everything's bigger in Alaska," he
said, running his hand down her hair, to soothe
rather than seduce. Which wasn't necessary since
she'd jumped him the moment they'd arrived
back at the cabin. Once she'd started singing at
the Gulch and their relationship had become
public, he'd begun spending the nights at the
cabin.

"So I've found," she agreed, placing her hand on the body part she was specifically referring to, which had the sheets tenting in response. They fit together, she thought. Not just their bodies but their minds. And hearts.

"About the he-who-shall-no-longer-be-named fiancé," she said. "I broke up with him because I found him cheating."

"I'm not surprised," Finn responded.

"Why not?"

He paused for a long moment, linked their fingers together, and lifted their joined hands up to his mouth. "Because you're not the type of woman who'd break a promise, even an engagement one, for a frivolous reason. Even if you didn't love the guy."

"That really sounds so cold-blooded," she muttered.

"More self-protective. Which I get. People have married for far less reasons than wanting a family."

"It was more than cheating," she said. "I probably, somewhere deep down, expected that since we'd never had any chemistry."

"Okay. I'm sorry you had to go through a rough break-up, but that's the best news I've heard all day."

She laughed, as he could always make her do. "I'm just going to tell this once. Then we're never going to discuss him or the topic again."

"Suits me fine." He began nibbling on her fingertips, as if she could have told him anything and it wouldn't matter. Because, although neither one of them had said the words out loud, she knew he loved her. As she'd come to love him.

"Short version, there was this woman he'd known all our lives. She was beautiful—"

"Not as beautiful as you."

"You can't know that."

"Of course I do. But we're not going to argue it, because the sooner we get it over with, the sooner we can get on to where I point out all the gorgeous, scenic stops on my Tori Cassidy tour."

She took a deep breath and willed her mind to focus even as her body began to respond to his nibbling mouth and words. "She married a much older man, solely for his fortune. Unfortunately, he stayed alive longer than expected."

He glanced up at her. "So they conspired to kill him?"

"No. If for no other reason than No Name wouldn't have the nerve. So, they had this long affair. Then finally Covington III, who has a strong sense of dynasty, gave him an ultimatum. If he didn't marry and start producing a new generation of heirs by the end of the year, he wouldn't get control of the cruise line and assorted other businesses. Which would mean that for the first time in a hundred years, an outsider would be brought in to take the helm."

"That'd be an incentive for some people."

"But not you." She leaned over and pressed a kiss against his lips. "Because you're not one of those rich, cheating billionaire playboys who only cares about spending money you did nothing to earn."

"No," he said, "that's not me. So, why were you chosen as the candidate?"

"That was accidental. He was with friends at a club where I was singing. He remembered my crush—"

"Which made you a sitting duck. So to speak."

"Exactly to speak. But not for the reason he thought, because, as I said, I was already over him. But I was also ready for a family, so his proposal seemed logical. He'd get what he wanted, and I'd get what I wanted. What I hadn't realized was that he planned to divorce me as soon as the business takeover was completed. That way, his mistress could divorce her husband without worrying about losing her prenup, because she'd still be marrying into money."

"Wow." Finn blew out a long breath. "Those two are really cold."

"As cold as this place probably gets in January," she agreed. "I only found out because I heard him talking to her the night before we were going off to Vegas to get married. Then we were coming straight up here."

"Why here? He doesn't seem—or sound, from what you've said—like a guy who'd get off on a frontier honeymoon."

"He wanted to get it done before his mother found out he was marrying me." And wasn't that the only part of the sordid story that hurt? Because it had reminded her of exactly how disposable she'd been considered.

"He never deserved you," Finn said. "Sounds like they deserve each other, and I hope the older guy lives forever." He drew her into his arms, then moved his body over hers. "So, they're forgotten?"

"Forgotten," she agreed, and followed him into a storm of their own making.

IT WAS HIS phone that woke them. Not the usual alarm but the tone signaling a call. Getting out of bed, Finn fumbled around in his jeans.

"I'm on my way," he said once he'd unearthed the phone. "I didn't realize I was on early shift this morning." For a guy who'd never missed a flight time, he was finding himself more and more distracted by Tori.

He'd made the decision, lying beside her, listening to her sleep, that he was going to trust his judgement, like Knox had advised, tell her that he loved her, and spill the beans about who he was.

He wasn't anything like IV. He and the fucking douchebag had nothing in common. Nothing. Zero. Zilch. Surely she'd understand that. And if she didn't immediately, he could win her over. He knew the reasons she'd guarded her heart, because his own were much the same. So, they could meet on common ground and work things through.

That was what he'd decided. He'd also come up with the idea of making her breakfast in bed beforehand. How hard could scrambled eggs, OJ, and toast be?

"You're not late," Mary said. "A plane disappeared last night. A Piper Navajo with a family of five disappeared on the way from Fairbanks to Wasilla. It was last seen flying over Nenana shortly before that storm hit."

"That's seventy-eight miles to here." With Denali in between.

"Exactly. Every charter airline's cancelling flights for today for the search. We'll do shifts. Everyone's working on divvying up the search area. I said we'd take between here and Healy." Which might only be twelve miles, but, like everything in Alaska, it was much larger than it sounded.

"What about the ELT?"

"Either it was too old to work or it didn't trigger," she said. Which could have been the case if it had crashed enough to damage the tail, where emergency locator transponders were usually placed.

"I'll be right in."

Tori, who'd heard the conversation, came back from the kitchen with a travel mug of coffee. "I can make up some breakfast for the searchers," she volunteered.

"Another plane went down right after I got up here," he said. "The Caribou took care of it, but Barbara Ann would probably appreciate the help."

"You go ahead and go," she said, rising up on her toes to kiss him. "I'll get ready and drive into town."

He paused. Then decided this was the worst moment to share his truth. Timing, Finn thought as he drove away, was everything.

MARY WAS BEHIND a long table made from pushing desks together, her schedule book in hand with a geographical map laid out in front of her. When she saw Finn come into the office, she came out from behind the table.

"I'm putting you with Yazz in one of the Cessnas," she said.

"Okay." Given that the other pilot had a lot

more experience with this landscape, that made sense. Her next words were, "He'll be your spotter. You'll be at the yoke." His surprise obviously showed on his face because she tacked on an explanation. "He had a few too many beers at the tree house raising," she said. "He's mostly fine, but I'm not letting him fly with a hangover. Besides, it works. He knows the terrain better than you. He can look for a plane in those creases and valleys you'd have no way of knowing about."

"Okay," Finn repeated. Years in the military had taught him to accept orders from superior officers. Which, under these circumstances, Mary was. He also knew that all the pilots in the office, even ones who didn't fly for Osprey, were *her* pilots. She cared for each and every one of them in the protective way a mama grizzly cared for her cubs.

"I also need to talk with you. Alone." She tilted her dark head toward the door to her private office.

"Something wrong?" Finn asked once she'd shut the door behind them.

"Did you tell her?"

Seriously? That was what was on her mind right now with a plane with a pilot and five passengers missing? "Not yet."

"Don't worry. I'm not going to hammer you on that because it would be a case of the tea kettle calling the frying pan black."

Finn wasn't even going to go there. Instead, he waited.

"First, you have to promise me that whatever I tell you won't get you upset."

"I flew a mission the day after I nearly drove a jet into the sea and found out my dad had died," Finn said. "If the U.S. Navy can trust me to get back into the air after that, I doubt there's anything you're going to say that'll prove a flight risk."

"Good point. So, since I don't want to risk you crashing out on that mountain, looking for a lost plane without knowing the truth, here goes." She drew in a deep breath. Blew it out. Then went through the sequence again while Finn struggled for patience. "Did you ever wonder why your father brought you up here that summer?"

"Sure. Especially since I'd never felt like a favorite son." That would've been James. At least looking in from the outside, which Finn had always been. "I figured, once we went up with Mike, that he knew I liked flying, so he decided I was the only one of his kids who'd enjoy it."

"That was part of it," she allowed. "Because it was in your blood."

"No way." Finn didn't want to talk about his relationship, or lack of it, with his father when there was a plane missing out there. "The only flying he ever did, that I can remember, was in his private jet."

"Not your father. Your uncle."

"My father was an only child." A thought suddenly struck like that thunderbolt that had shaken the cabin last night. "Are you talking about Mike?"

"He was Colin's half-brother," she confirmed. "Your grandfather Brannigan had come up here fishing, and gotten a local girl pregnant. Since she was a native, there was no way he was going to take her back to the lower forty-eight. So he just left."

"Like that? He didn't even arrange to take care of his child?" Mike Muldoon, he thought. The man who could've lived in the air. Just like him.

"Appears not. Anyway, since we're on the clock here, fast forward to the year your mother died. Your grandfather's lawyer's son was going through his father's office, in order to clean things out to move to a new place, when he found a codicil to his original will, leaving a bequest to a Mike Muldoon.

"Your father, being curious, came up here and met Mike. The two hit it off, right away, partly because Mike had had a good life and wasn't one to hold grudges, but more importantly, Colin finally understood why you'd been drawing planes since you were old enough to hold a crayon.

Blood tells, I remember him saying.

"Even after your mother passed, although he didn't know how to show it, he cared for all his boys. Deep down, family was the most important thing to Colin. Which is why he came up here every year to spend two weeks with his brother. Who didn't want to be acknowledged, because, quite honestly, Mike didn't want to land in the Brannigan spotlight."

"Which was why Dad came up here under an assumed name," Finn said.

"In the beginning, I suspect Colin didn't want Mike to know who he was. But yeah, after the first few days, when he admitted who he was and they got along like gangbangers, he kept the ruse up because it allowed him to be himself, away from the image *his* father had originally created and he'd built on.

"He waited until you were old enough to appreciate flying in these mountains to bring you up here to meet your uncle. But I have to tell you that, every summer, we'd hear about all your accomplishments. Both before and after that trip. He was proud as punch about you."

Even as his head was being hammered with this generations-old family secret, Finn noted that, for once, Mary had gotten the phrase right.

"Well." He nodded, deciding he'd chew on all this later. "Thank you for telling me that." He would not allow himself to be furious at his father for having kept him from getting to know his uncle. Didn't he know, firsthand, how difficult some secrets were to share? And wow, his father's was a doozie. "I'd better get out there."

"Be careful," she said as they left the room. "You've got a woman waiting for you."

Finn hoped.

25

ONE THING FINN had discovered about flying in Alaska was that, one minute, blue skies went on forever, then the next, Mother Nature could slap out a giant grizzly paw and remind you who ruled these mountains.

He and Yazz had been in the air for about twenty minutes, after reaching a comfortable cruising altitude, when a sudden wind blew off the face of the mountain, bringing with it a black cloud that shot out rain like bullets.

"Shit," Yazz muttered. "It's as dark as a December midnight. Let's go back along the lake's coastline to see if we can get some clearance."

Since they were flying under VFR (visual flight rules), Finn dropped to eight hundred feet, which was low even for a bush plane. Low enough to see beavers lumbering along the rocky beach and seagulls picking at a dead salmon. "Odds are against finding the plane here," Finn said.

"True. But at least we've got enough visibility

not to crash into the side of the mountain. That's all the team needs. To be out looking for us. There should be a valley up ahead. Shoot for it."

Three minutes later, Finn found the cut blocked with another wall of dense clouds. "Not going to happen," he said, banking a hundred and eighty degrees and turning back the way they'd come. With any luck, the wind would've blown away the clouds behind them.

The radio traffic picked up, pilots reporting both clearances and clouds, but no sign of the Navajo. "I'm going to try to follow the river," Finn said. "If I were in trouble, that's what I'd do."

"Might as well give it a try."

He dropped even lower, pushing the ceiling limits at six hundred feet. The lower level was safer, but it was like being back home in California, trying to get from Burbank to San Diego using side roads instead of the freeway. He'd throttled back to save fuel, but that also slowed him down, which could be trouble if they suddenly came upon a hill covered with tall trees.

For the first time since landing in Caribou, he was missing his carrier deck.

"That's why I chose the Air Force," Yazz said when Finn shared that thought with him. "Unlike you Navy flyboys, we were smart enough to build long, straight, flat runways that don't run away from us."

Finn couldn't argue that. "Right now I'd just settle for some blue sky."

And then, as if taking pity on him, the granite clouds parted like in some old Bible movie in a way that had Finn almost expecting to see Moses on the mountain, holding up a pair of golden tablets.

He exchanged a look with his spotter. "Maybe," Yazz suggested dryly, "you could have asked for that about thirty minutes ago?"

They continued on, following the river through a saddle in the mountain, over meadows and lakes and rocky uplifts. They'd been in the air a little over two hours when Finn started doing the math. Under optimum conditions, the Cessna had enough fuel for three hours of flying, but these conditions were less than optimal. He'd been fighting headwinds much of the way, which ate up fuel, and no pilot, whatever he was flying, would ever head home with the idea of having just enough. The rule was to always keep more in the tank than needed.

"Five more minutes," he said. "Then we're going back."

"Works for me," his spotter, who knew these mountains far better than Finn did, agreed. They'd just crested over another rise when they spotted the plane, caught up in some trees next to a lake.

"Well, it didn't break apart," Yazz observed.

"Or burn," Finn said, thinking back on the sight of his Hornet exploding into a fireball over another very different range of mountains.

He swooped lower to get another look while Yazz called in their position for a fresh plane to come retrieve them. Given the timbered terrain, he suggested a floatplane.

The pilot and passengers had cut up what Finn guessed to be clothes and spelled out *SOS. All OK* on the rocky ground. When he saw three kids, two adults that had to be the parents, and the pilot all jumping up and down waving their arms, he dove lower, circled three times, and wagged his wings to let them know he'd seen them and would send help. Then, mission accomplished, headed back for home.

✧   ✧   ✧

TORI WAS GOING crazy. Although everyone else in the place seemed amazingly calm under the circumstances, she'd been listening to the radio calls that reported hard wind, dense clouds, and rain. For the first time the mountain, which Kendra had painted in such pretty sugar colors, which greeted her every morning with a dazzling view, whose flowered meadows she'd seen from the air, and whose trails she'd hiked in her new red boots, took on an entirely new character. It had turned dangerously malevolent, like the Misty Mountains in *The Hobbit*, inhabited by goblins and rock-throwing giants.

"He'll be okay," Mary assured her over and over again. It didn't help.

She was finally able to breathe when she heard Finn's voice, sounding no different from when he'd first flown her here from Anchorage, saying that they were headed home. But she still wasn't going to fully relax until she saw the Cessna taxiing up the runway to the hangar.

The place had broken out in applause when Yazz reported they'd found the plane, with all aboard safe and waiting for a pickup. Jackie Johnson, a sixty-something native who Mary had told her had practically grown up flying planes, had taken off in the Beaver to fetch them.

"Not a bad day's work for a billionaire's kid," a grizzled old man Tori remembered being the owner of Caribou's hardware store drawled.

"He's a former naval aviator," she corrected politely.

The room had gone as silent as a church on Sunday morning. Oddly, no one was looking at anyone else. Only Mary was looking at her. The sympathy in her eyes said it all.

It couldn't be! Tori realized that disbelief and denial must be written all over her face when the man, Doug something, she recalled, drove his point home. "His old man, Colin Brannigan, used to come up here every summer. One year he brought one of his kids. Though he's grown up, I recognized him right away. He looks like his old man. And his uncle. Who took him flying."

Uncle? But Mike Muldoon had taken Finn flying.

"It's true," Mary said quietly. "Colin Brannigan and Mike were half brothers."

Could this day get any worse? Why didn't anyone in the room seem surprised by that?

"And Finn knew?" And had told her the story about owing Mary and never mentioned that she was his aunt by marriage? Because then, the thought hit home through her whirling mind, he'd have to admit to being a member of one of the wealthiest, most famous families in the country. Far wealthier, she suspected, than the Covingtons.

"Not until today," Mary admitted. "Colin wanted to keep his identity a secret." She shot a hot, accusing glare at the man who'd blown up Tori's life. In front of what appeared to be half the town. Along with a TV news crew from Anchorage.

"Secrecy seems to run in the family," Tori managed as she realized the final betrayal. She'd learned over the years that the most effective lies were wrapped in enough truth to give them credibility. Finn had told her he'd grown up in Calabasas. Carter had grown up in a mansion in Holmby Hills. Los Angeles might be huge and sprawling, but such wealth was concentrated in the hands of a privileged few. Their paths had to have crossed.

"I need to leave," she told Mary.

"I understand," the older woman said. "I'll walk out with you."

Since you could have heard the proverbial pin drop, Tori wasn't going to create a scene by arguing. She just walked out the door, Mary following close behind.

"He didn't mean to lie," the older woman said.

"He certainly did a good job of it." Tori's blood was cold. Her heart was colder. Which was a good thing, she decided. If it was frozen, it couldn't bleed all over the ground and humiliate her further.

"He didn't lie about his name," Mary said. "He just didn't tell anyone about his family."

"That man, Doug, knew."

"Doug is an ass. He enjoys pulling people's chains. I don't know when he figured it out. And I didn't realize he knew about Mike until he hinted at it at the tree house building party."

"Finn knew how I felt." Tori clicked the fob

on her keychain, opening the rental car's door.

"Which is probably why he was having a harder time telling you the longer it went on," Mary pressed his case. "It was obvious to anyone in town that he's over the moon for you."

"I appreciate your feelings for him," Tori said. "But I really don't want to talk about him anymore."

The sound of an engine got her attention. Glancing up, she saw the red-and-white plane approaching the landing strip.

Telling herself that she was *not* running way, Tori got into the car, started the engine, and drove out of the parking lot.

She did not look back.

26

DAMN. FINN CURSED himself all the way out to the cabin. Mary had been right. He should have told Tori before she'd found out from someone else. Before he'd made love to her. Hell, he should have told her right off the bat.

Though, he argued, what was he supposed to do that night in the Del? Introduce himself and say, "And by the way, I just happen to be Colin Brannigan's youngest son"?

When he'd spent his life trying to be anything but the old man's son.

And yet...

He thought about what his brothers said about his father having always loved his mother from when they'd first met as teenagers. Then later, when they'd reconnected, the bond had been strong enough to marry and have a family. A loving family, he realized. He couldn't remember that night she'd died. The Monopoly game or that week she'd spent in a coma and he hadn't been allowed to visit her.

It had all been gone in a heartbeat. The sunshine and happiness that, every once in a while, he thought he could remember. More since he'd been with Tori. And not just because there were times when she reminded him of his mother. No, it was more than that.

She made him feel like Kathleen Hayes must have made Colin Brannigan, who'd been orphaned himself as a boy, feel. She'd made his father whole again. Filled those cold, empty places in what had to have been a lonely heart.

And then she'd been taken away from him but, according to his brothers' stories this past year, he'd never forgotten. Enough that the others all believed that when their father had sent them out on that quest to find themselves, he'd also intended them to find a love that completed each of his sons the way Kathleen had completed him. The way Tori had Finn. And he knew that he'd done for her.

"You can fix this," Finn assured himself as he drove up to the cabin. "You can make it right."

Because failure was not an option.

TORI HAD KNOWN he would be coming. She'd thought she'd been prepared, had steeled her ripped-to-shreds heart against him. A heart that disobeyed her command and leaped in joy at the sight of him standing in her outer doorway.

"I can explain," he said, his hands shoved deeply into his pockets.

His handsome face looked drawn. As if he hadn't gotten any sleep. Which, to be fair, because of having spent the night with her and that early phone call, he probably hadn't. And it had to have been stressful, trying to find that missing family, with those little children, and fighting the mountain weather, and...

No! Stop feeling sorry for him! He's a liar who doesn't deserve it.

She lifted a shoulder in what she hoped would look like an uncaring shrug. "Mary already told me."

"Did she tell you that I love you?"

"No." *Stop that!* she told her foolish heart that had switched from jumping for joy to practically melting into a little puddle.

"I do."

"Well, thank you. That's nice to hear. But it doesn't change anything."

"Change anything from when Doug decided to stick his finger into something that had nothing to do with him? Or change how you felt with me this morning? Or yesterday? Or two nights ago when I was painting your toenails to match your fingernails because you hadn't wanted to spend the extra bucks on a pedicure at Midnight Sun?"

Now, dammit, her toes joined in with her heart and began to curl at the sensual memory.

"And you know what?" he said. "I know you love me, too."

"It doesn't matter."

"Why not?"

"Because neither of us is any good at this."

"What?"

"You don't let anyone in. Neither do I."

"You're wrong. I let you so far in I can't tell where you leave off and I begin. We're like this." He lifted his hands, linking his long, dark fingers together. Then tugged, showing they wouldn't separate.

"Yet you wouldn't tell me who you really were."

"I let you know everything about who I was," he countered. "Hell, more than I've shared with anyone. Ever. Even my brothers. The only thing I didn't tell you was my name."

"And that you're rich."

"My father was rich. I'm not."

"Yet for some reason, your Wikipedia bio doesn't show you're Colin Brannigan's son. Why is that?"

"That's an easy one. When I was flying over Afghanistan, I had to eject to avoid getting blown up by a missile. While I was alone out in those mountains for two very long nights, hoping to get rescued before the bad guys got to me first, the military called my brother, James, who I'd listed as my PNOK, which is militaryspeak for primary next of kin. He used the Brannigan media contacts to make sure no one leaked my name. Then the military sent some high-level hackers in to scrub any Internet citation, because everyone thought I'd make a too valuable captive target that could be used for propaganda."

"I hate the idea that happened to you." She might be hurt and feeling humiliated, but comparatively, what he'd been through out there in that hostile land, had to have been much, much worse.

"I came back," he said. "A lot of guys didn't."

She had to give Finn reluctant points for not playing a hero card. But that didn't change the fact that he'd kept so much from her. "Who owns Osprey?"

"I do," he admitted what she'd already guessed on the way home from the airfield. "But I don't want it. I inherited it when my father died of cancer last September and tried to give it to Mary, but she refused. She insisted that Dad left it to me for a reason. But she runs it like she always has, because I don't want anything to do with the goddamn business," he said on a flare of frustration she'd never witnessed from him.

"I just want to fly… And spend the rest of my life with you. Here in Caribou or California or Timbuktu. It doesn't matter. If you want to keep traveling the world, that works for me. Because anyplace will feel like home as long as you're there with me."

She was so tempted. He was offering her everything she'd ever wanted. Love, a family. A home. But the simple fact was that she didn't, couldn't trust it.

"I can't." She shook her head. "I let myself care too much, Finn. You're right. It wasn't a hookup. Or even a fling. It's something deeper. More complicated. And neither one of us does that."

"You don't know that we can't."

"And you don't know that we can."

"So that's it?" He ran a hand over his short hair. "Here's your coat, Sailor, don't let the door hit your ass on the way out?"

It wasn't just fatigue etched into his face. It was frustration and something else she couldn't quite define. *Desperation*?

"I'm sorry."

"Don't feel like the Lone Fucking Ranger," he shot back. "What do you want me to do to make this right, Tori? Do you want me to beg? I'll get down on my knees right now."

Amazingly, he did drop right down onto them in that small outer foyer. Which, while she enjoyed reading about the hero groveling at the end of a romance novel, before the couple walked hand in hand into their sunny happily ever after, only made her feel worse.

"Finn…"

"Do you want me to strip naked and crawl down Front Street at high noon? Because, hey, just say the word, and I'm there. Hell, Barbara Ann will probably be happy to sell tickets."

"Please. I don't want you to do anything like that. I'm not even angry anymore."

He got back onto his feet and looked down at her. "I'm not giving up," he warned her. "Also, this is lousy timing, but I have something for you. It came yesterday Fedex. I was going to give it to you earlier, then Mary called about that crash." He reached into his jacket pocket, pulled out an envelope and held it out to her.

"What's this?" she asked suspiciously. But she did take it.

"A letter from Kevin Osborne, CEO of Pegasus Records, which happens to be a subsidiary of Spotlight Pictures, which is, yes, another Brannigan company. He bought your contract, but before he re-releases your songs, he wants to negotiate another, better contract. Apparently you got robbed, which isn't that much of a surprise, since if your old company had been any good, they probably wouldn't have gone under. You need to have your agent call him."

"I don't know what to say." He'd gone behind her back. But how could she be angry at him for handing her her dream?

"You don't have to say anything. Hell, you can toss it away, if you want. But I think you're too damn smart to let any feelings for me get in the way of reclaiming your career.

"Meanwhile, I'm willing to give you some space, because I don't know what else to say. Well, I did think of something driving over here, but it sounds as if I'm cribbing from Hollywood to win you over."

He gave her a long look that settled on her lips, which took on their own mind and parted slightly, totally undermining the point she'd been trying to make.

"You complete me, Tori Cassidy. And yeah, it sounds phony and sappy and clichéd. But it's fucking true."

Having made his point, he turned and walked away.

Just as she'd done at the airfield, he did not look back.

27

"WHAT THE HELL are you thinking?" Zoe asked when Tori had called to tell her what had happened. "From what you've told me, he's perfect."

"I thought he was. But he's rich."

"Oh, boy. That would sure as hell be a deal breaker for me. Not every rich guy is like Carter Covington IV. Look at John F. Kennedy, Jr."

"He's dead. He died in a plane crash. Which could happen to Finn."

"So, that's the part that's keeping you from committing?"

"No. It's dangerous. But people can get hit by a bus crossing the street." Or by a drunk driver coming home from a luau. Or by a teenager while you were out getting ice cream for family night. Life, she'd learned, could be cruelly random.

"It's not the money. Because you said he doesn't want it. Do you think he's lying about that?"

"No."

"And let's not forget here, he went to the trouble to salvage your career from what was a flaming dumpster. And from what I can tell, he didn't do it to make you forgive him, because he already had the letter from Pegasus. Which, if you weren't my BFF, I'd be really jealous about, because that's like hitting all the Powerball numbers. You are going to accept it, aren't you?"

"I'd be a fool to turn it down."

"Of course you would. And you've never been a fool. A little misguided, perhaps, when it came to IV the douche, but you're not stupid. So, what's the problem?"

"I'm scared, okay?" Tori heard herself shouting. It was the truth she hadn't wanted to face. She was terrified of being broken. Which she knew, deep in her wounded heart, Finn would never do.

"Well, then," Zoe said. "That's an easy fix."

"How?"

"Get over it. And since you're going to be rich, I'll expect first-class tickets to come up there and play maid-of-honor for this wedding. Now go make his day and tell the poor guy you forgive him."

With that tough-love advice, she hung up.

✧   ✧   ✧

FINN HADN'T BEEN in any mood to leave the house and go down to the Gold Gulch. After taking a long, hot shower to take the nervous sweat stink off, he'd put on a pair of sweats and was planning to get slowly and methodically drunk.

Then tomorrow, he'd war-game how to get Tori Cassidy to marry him. Because damned if he was going to be the only Brannigan brother to end up alone.

But before he could even finish the first glass of whiskey, Barbara Ann had called to tell him that all the power had gone out in the bar. When he suggested she call an electrician, she told him the one in Healy couldn't get to her for two days. And there was no point in him telling her to call the hardware store, because she currently wasn't speaking to Doug after what he'd done.

So, he'd driven to town and walked into the Gulch, where the older woman had said she'd be waiting on him. The place was as dark as she'd told him. He might not be an electrician, but anyone could check some circuit breakers.

"Anyone here?" he called out into the darkness.

"Just me," a voice said.

A moment later, a single spotlight turned on, revealing Tori perched on a stool, dressed in a short black denim skirt that revealed a mouth-watering amount of smooth, long leg and a sweater that fit like it had been sprayed on.

"I realized after you left that I hadn't played you my new song," she said.

"Okay." Finn wasn't exactly sure what was going on, but he wasn't going to complain that she was talking to him.

She strummed a few chords on her Taylor. Then began to sing.

Love has never been an easy game,
I always lose the final round.
Home has never been a certain place,
It always moves when I start to settle down.

As it always did, her voice went straight from her lips directly to the center of his heart.

I have sailed to every distant sea,
I leave love before love can leave me.
It feels much easier to lose than keep,
These dreams of home.

Afraid to spook her but unable to keep his distance, he began to move across the room, weaving his way through the tables.

Carry me home, carry me home,
Carry me home, carry me home.

She slid off the stool and stood there bathed in that sole spotlight, looking straight at him as she moved on to the next verse.

My foolish heart is like a gypsy wind,
A lonely ship, a skipping stone.
Tossed by lovers' lies and promises,
Fated to wander and to roam.

He'd nearly reached the small stage when Tori put the guitar down and began walking toward him.

Then I found you in the wilderness,
You melted years of ice with just one kiss.
Beneath the tough skin of our surfaces,
We found a home.
Carry me home, carry me home,
Carry me home, carry me home.

They'd met in the middle, just as they'd done in life. Two lost souls, Finn thought, seeking their other half. And amazingly, finding it in this remote place at the near top of the world.

You feel like the sunlight,
Of my childhood days.

She went into his arms and wrapped hers around his neck, going up on her toes to bring her lips a whisper from his.

When love filled up my family,
And family kept me safe.

Her lips brushed against his. "Carry me home, carry me home," she sang softly as she pressed kisses over the seam of his mouth. "Carry me home."

Although, like his mom, he'd never been accused of being able to carry a tune, Finn sang along with her. Because the song wasn't just Tori's song. It was his, as well. In her, he'd found his true home.

"Carry me home." Their joined voices carried over to the doorway to the café, where Barbara Ann and Mary stood in the shadows, their eyes misting.

"You did good," Mary murmured, keeping her voice low. Not that it mattered, since she could have been shouting at the top of her lungs, and the couple swaying in the center of the Gold Gulch couldn't have heard her, lost in their own world as they were.

"I'm mayor," Barbara Ann reminded her. "It's my job to take care of my people. Plus, I wasn't about to lose a great performer. I think I'll put that ad back out for a new cook. She's too good to be stuck back there in the kitchen where no one but John Black can hear her sing."

"Carry me home. Carry me home."

The last note hung in the hushed air like a prayer. A promise.

Finn drew back his head and brushed the moisture from her cheeks.

"I thought you never cried," he said.

"I don't." She smiled up at him through her tears. "These are happy tears. I'm so sorry, Finn—"

"It's done. We've weathered our first storm. Had our first fight. Now what would you say if I carried you home to my place where we can spend the rest of the day in bed making up? And, since I want to spend the rest of my life with you, checking out how soon we can get married?"

"I'd say yes," she said on a joyous laugh as he lifted her off her feet and carried her out of the saloon.

Epilogue

ALTHOUGH FINN WOULD have preferred to get married right away, he should have realized that Barbara Ann would insist on a full-out Southern shindig. Needless to say, her partner in crime, and, it had turned out, Finn's aunt by marriage, Mary, was right there with her. And if that wasn't bad enough, his aunt, Claire, who'd been in contact with both of them by Skype, flew up two weeks early to help the other two females put on the finishing touches.

They held the wedding in the house where Finn and Tori had been living and where they'd turned one of the rooms into a studio for her to record her new album for Pegasus Records.

Thanks to the numerous bedrooms and guesthouse, there was room for Claire, as well as all six of his brothers and their wives and fiancées, making Finn wonder yet again if their father had originally built the house with family reunions in mind. Although his brothers had initially been stunned to discover they'd had a secret uncle, Mary's warm welcome to her native Alaska had smoothed over what could have been an uncomfortable situation.

Now, while their women were in the master suite with Tori's best friend, Zoe, who'd flown up from L.A., fussing over the bride, Finn gathered with his brothers in the study. It was a decidedly masculine room, with heavy leather furniture, a towering river-rock fireplace, and paneled walls lined with books. The fact that the books all seemed well read revealed that Colin Brannigan had done more than fishing during his annual visits to Caribou. The idea of his father slowing down enough to relax was something Finn was still wrapping his head around, but if there was one thing this past year had proven, it was that there was a great deal about their father none of them had known.

"I realize it's customary to toast the groom," Finn said. "But we Brannigans have always had our own way of doing things, so I'm going to mix it up."

He saw James's brows arch as he pulled out a bottle of Villa Pietro Rosso Riserva from a cabinet. "Knox ordered this for me from the Positano winery our big brother inherited," he said. "I thought it would be a good change from the Bushmills. A new toasting drink for our generation."

He opened the bottle, then poured the wine into the heavy Waterford glasses he'd already set out. In the sunlight streaming through the floor-to-ceiling windows, the rich red color gleamed like rubies. When each of them had a glass, he lifted his.

"To Dad," he said, "who sent us each on a journey to find ourselves, knowing that once we did, we'd become open to the type of forever-after love he was fortunate to have shared with Mom for so many years.

"And while our individual quests proved a reward in themselves, they brought us back to family. So, also here's to brotherhood, and to the future generations of Brannigans, which, one of us, being an annoying overachiever, has already gotten a head start on."

He grinned at James, whose fiancée had arrived from Positano with a cute baby bump. His formerly staid, workaholic brother grinned back, his face beaming with paternal pride.

All seven brothers lifted their glasses and drank to the man who'd changed their lives over the past twelve months. And to each other.

Then, united, they moved to the sunroom, where Finn went to the head of the white runner and stood, awaiting his bride.

Although he knew every inch of Tori's body,

he was still stunned at the sight of her walking down that aisle in a strapless white gown fit for a fairy-tale princess. She'd pulled her hair up, which accentuated that sexy slant of her gypsy dark eyes. When she reached his side, she smiled up at him, and as Finn knew it would still do when they were old and gray watching their great-grandchildren jumping into the lake outside the window, his heart took a now-familiar tumble.

The vows were both simple and timeless.

To love. Honor. Cherish.

Without taking his gaze from hers, with hands far steadier than his heart, Finn slipped the ring onto Tori's finger. Her eyes, moist with happy tears, placed the gleaming symbol of promise on his.

"You may kiss the bride," the priest, who'd come to Caribou from Our Lady of Guadalupe in nearby Healy, announced.

"About time," Knox said, earning a laugh from the others.

Finn lowered his head, and as their lips touched for the first time as man and wife, an audible sigh could be heard rippling through the guests.

Then, hands linked, Finn and Tori Brannigan walked down the white runner to Tori's "Carry Me Home," which was playing from the hidden speakers, into the arms of their friends and family.

✧   ✧   ✧

Dear Readers, I hope you enjoyed this collaborative series 7 Brides for 7 Brothers. I had a grand time collaborating on these seven sexy brothers' love stories with such wonderfully talented, bestselling authors Barbara Freethy, Ruth Cardello, Melody Anne, Christie Ridgway, Lynn Raye Harris, and Roxanne St. Claire!

For those of you who might be new to my books, I hope you'll check out my other books at my website. Also, while on my site, you can listen to fabulous singer/songwriter Jasper Lepak's "Carry Me Home," which she wrote for Tori, on the book's page. bit.ly/7BridesFor7BrothersFinn

✧   ✧   ✧

Did you miss the beginning of the Brannigan Brothers series? Start with LUKE, from New York Times bestselling author Barbara Freethy.

Luke Brannigan lives for the adrenaline rush, which makes his job as a filmmaker of extreme sporting adventures the perfect career choice. He loves to travel the world, risking life and limb to capture the most amazing shot. Some might say he's running away from something… or someone.

When Luke's billionaire father Colin Brannigan dies unexpectedly, Luke is shocked to receive title to

the mountain lodge where his parents first met. Having been estranged from his father for years, Luke has no idea why his dad picked him to inherit this very personal piece of property... until he realizes the pretty blonde manager is Lizzie Parker, his former college girlfriend.

Luke and Lizzie have an emotional and heart-breaking past, but will they have a future? Will love be Luke's greatest adventure yet?

Other Books from JoAnn Ross

The Shelter Bay series
The Homecoming
One Summer
On Lavender Lane
Moonshell Beach
Sea Glass Winter
Castaway Cove
You Again
Beyond the Sea (pre-publication title, A Sea Change)
Sunset Point
Christmas in Shelter Bay, 2017

The Castlelough series
A Woman's Heart
Fair Haven
Legends Lake
Briarwood Cottage
Beyond the Sea

River's Bend Series
River's Bend (Cooper's story)
Long Road Home (Sawyer's story) Pre-publication was
Hot Shot

Orchid Island Series
Sun Kissed

7 BRIDES for 7 Brothers Series
Finn—7 Brides for 7 Brothers (Book 7)

Rum Runner Island Series
A Place in Time
Somewhere in Time, 2017

About The Author

JoAnn Ross wrote her first novella—a tragic romance about two star-crossed mallard ducks—for a second grade writing assignment.

The paper earned a gold star.

And JoAnn kept writing.

She's now written around one hundred novels (she quit keeping track long ago), has been published in twenty-six countries, and is a member of the Romance Writers of America's Honor Roll of best-selling authors. Two of her titles have been excerpted in *Cosmopolitan* magazine and her books have also been published by the Doubleday, Rhapsody, Literary Guild, and Mystery Guild book clubs.

JoAnn lives with her husband and two fuzzy rescued dogs, who pretty much rule the house, in the Pacific Northwest.

Sign up to receive the latest news from JoAnn
joannross.com/newsletter

Visit JoAnn's Website
www.joannross.com

Like JoAnn on Facebook
facebook.com/JoAnnRossbooks

Follow JoAnn on Goodreads
goodreads.com/author/show/31311.JoAnn_Ross

Follow JoAnn on Pinterest
pinterest.com/JoAnnRossBooks

Follow JoAnn on Instagram
instagram.com/joannrossbooks

Made in the USA
Lexington, KY
03 March 2017